The Avenging Nun

While she was gazing over the brick parapet, she'd gradually become aware of another presence on the roof. The realization of this had sent a chill through her. Then she turned and, standing there behind her, was a weird-looking figure in a gray habit and cowl which hid the face.

It took her only a second to decide who it was. The avenging Nun of Valencia! The ghost of the nun who had become blind as a result of her dedicated efforts illuminating the pages of the Book of Gospels in long-ago Spain. The phantom reached out a hand toward her, and she saw that the hand was a skeleton hand, bones without flesh! She let out a cry of fear and edged along the roof top in an effort to get to the door leading down into the building and her route to escape.

But the gray menace of the Nun of Valencia followed her and kept between her and the door. Gradually the phantom moved nearer to her, until at last one of the bony hands reached out and grasped her by the wrist!

The House on Mount Vernon Street

W.E.D. Ross

AVON
PUBLISHERS OF BARD, CAMELOT, DISCUS, EQUINOX AND FLARE BOOKS

AVON BOOKS
A division of
The Hearst Corporation
959 Eighth Avenue
New York, New York 10019

Published by arrangement with Lenox Hill Press.

First Avon Printing, January, 1974.

Printed in the U.S.A.

To my good friends:
ROLLO and ALICE SILVER,
who are book collectors and who live on Mount Vernon Street, but who bear no resemblance to the much less nice people in this book.

The House on Mount Vernon Street

CHAPTER ONE

The first time Clare Rand saw the house on Mount Vernon Street was on a foggy night in October. She'd arrived from Chicago to land at Boston's Logan Airport and then had taken a cab for the short ride to the Beacon Hill area and the old house. She'd traveled light, carrying only one overnight bag, as she'd sent her other luggage ahead by Railway Express. She was going to make her home in Boston for some time, and so it had been a permanent move.

She paid the cabby and then, as he drove off in the fog to make a turn at the Charles Street corner close by, she studied the ancient red brick house with its trim white shutters and interesting iron-railed steps. It was a narrow house, but it rose four stories above the street and had the kind of grace one finds only in houses especially designed for private owners. Whoever had commissioned the house to be built had known exactly what they wanted.

For the moment she was worried about the reception she would receive from her Uncle Benjamin Rand and his second wife, Winifred. Her Uncle Benjamin had written a series of pleading letters urging her to give up her job and come to Boston and live with him. The several notes she'd received from his much younger wife had not been so warmly inviting. But in the end Clare had decided to accept her uncle's invitation. Aside from his wife, she was his only heir. And as he had said, it was time they knew each other.

A hippie, a man in suede with a long beard and lots of fringe on his jacket, came by with a girl in a granny dress of dark green on his arm. They were heading down the steep incline of Mount Vernon Street for the thoroughly mod world of Charles Street. Here, within a short walk from the center of downtown Boston, was the Greenwich Village of the one-time Athens of America. The two gave her curious stares and moved on.

She still hesitated with her bag in hand. It was eight in the evening, and she had no idea whether her Uncle Benjamin would be on hand to greet her or not. The strange thing was that she didn't even know what he looked like. They'd exchanged snapshots, but the one of him had been of a slim elderly gentleman bent over a bed of roses in his flower garden, with only a scant view of his features, while hers had been of a laughing girl standing on the beach with the sun in her eyes. Uncle Benjamin probably thought she suffered from a perpetual squint.

As a matter of record, she didn't. Her eyes were wide, green and frank, to match her auburn hair and rather boyish yet attractive face. She was not the winsome type and didn't pretend to be. For some time she'd been on her own. After her father's death while she was in her teens, her mother had remarried and gone to California. This left Clare, just out of business school, obliged to find both a job and a place to live. She located a job in an advertising agency and found a place to live with two other girls from the agency in a shared apartment. It had worked well enough, but she'd been tiring of it when she'd heard from her uncle.

It was characteristic of him that he'd used a private detective agency to find her. Her family had not been in contact with him for years. The trouble began with a quarrel between her father and his older brother about an inheritance years before. Benjamin had gotten the major share of the legacy of a cousin, and in the bitterness the two had parted, never to meet again as long as they lived.

Her father had never spoken of her Uncle Benjamin. She knew vaguely that he existed, but to all purposes he might have been an inhabitant of another planet. She and the uncle she had not met lived in worlds far removed. After her father's death and her mother's remarriage, she'd been approached by a representative of her uncle. It had come as a complete surprise. She learned that her Uncle Benjamin lived in Boston, was a book collector and immensely wealthy. None of these things were of more than casual interest to her, but the fact that he wanted her to come and live with him as a kind of adopted daughter was.

She exchanged a number of letters with him and came to enjoy the precise messages written in a fine, rather cramped hand. During this time she contemplated the difference acceptance of his offer would make in her life. Her job was good but not that important. She had no steady boyfriend and no really close friends in Chicago. She could make the move without any change in her manner of living, and so she decided to try it.

She was staring up through the fog at the shining white-painted door with its rich panels and fine brasswork. She could no longer put off the moment of truth, so there was nothing to do but advance up the stairs and touch the bell.

After a nervous moment of waiting, the door was opened by a large, rather dour woman with horn-rimmed glasses. She said, "Yes?"

"I'm Clare Rand," Clare said. "My uncle is expecting me."

"Oh, yes!" the woman said without obvious warmth. "Your uncle and aunt are out for a while. They said to make yourself comfortable. Your uncle's secretary is here. You can talk to him." The woman stood aside and opened the door.

Clare went in. The hall was tastefully decorated with fine colonial wallpaper and a varied selection of excellent prints. There was a door to the left leading to the drawing room and stairs directly up from the door which probably led to the sleeping quarters of the old mansion.

The woman said, "I'm Mrs. Fox, the housekeeper. I'll show you up to your room. Your other things arrived yesterday, and we put them up there, though we made no attempt to unpack them."

"Naturally not," Clare said. "I'm happy to meet you, Mrs. Fox."

"Yes," the big woman said absently. "I'll show you to your room now. It's on the fourth floor. You'll have noticed the house is narrow, though it does extend back a long way to the gardens. We're very fortunate to have the gardens."

"I know," she said. "I have a snapshot of my Uncle Benjamin working at a rose bed."

"He gives it a lot of his time in season," Mrs. Fox said. "It's good for him." She started to lead the way upstairs, talking at the same time. "The library and other book storage rooms occupy all the second floor; also, there are rooms in the cellars with stored books. The third floor comprises your aunt's and uncle's sleeping quarters and an upstairs parlor where your aunt often reads or entertains. The other bedrooms are all on the fourth floor."

They passed the second floor and took a narrower flight of stairs up to the next level. This in turn gave way to a still narrower and steeper flight of steps which opened on a long dark hall which ran all the way back to the rear of the house. There were doors opening off the left side of it at intervals, and Clare guessed these would be the upstairs bedrooms.

It turned out that she was right, and hers was the second one down along the hall. From its window she had a view of Charles Street and the river beyond. It was lighted by an old-fashioned ceiling fixture, though there was a bedside table lamp and a lamp on the dresser. The bed was a four-poster, and the other furniture in the room was of the style of a century before. Attractive green drapes decorated the good-sized French window. It had a shadowy atmosphere which Clare liked, since it suggested rest and quiet.

Mrs. Fox indicated the luggage neatly stacked in one corner of the large room. "You'll be wanting to get at that tomorrow."

"Yes," Clare said with a smile. "I don't think I'll try to cope with all that unpacking tonight."

"No," the housekeeper said. "When you're settled, come downstairs. Mr. Carney will be glad to see you. He's your uncle's private secretary."

"Thank you," Clare said.

Mrs. Fox hesitated at the door. "Have you had your evening meal?"

"Yes. They served it on the plane. I don't want more to eat now."

"Very well," the big woman with the horn-rimmed glasses said. "If you want anything else, let me know."

"I will, and thanks," Clare said. Mrs. Fox went out, and she moved about the room, inspecting it. The furnishings were drab, but they were expensive and in good taste. The whole house spoke of money and plenty of it. Why had Uncle Benjamin wanted her to return and share it? Bad conscience, perhaps, or maybe a feeling of lonesomeness for someone of his own family and the desire to do a good deed.

She put her overnight bag on the table and unpacked it. When she'd done this and freshened up, she decided it was time to go down and see her uncle's secretary. The idea of a male secretary was new to her, and she visualized him as some elderly retired worker now employed by Uncle Benjamin to care for his books.

She left her room and went down the two flights of stairs to the second floor. As she started down the final flight of stairs, she could see the entrance to the large, high-ceilinged library with wood-paneling and a wealth of books. And at a desk by the front window of the room, at the far end of it from her, was a handsome, slender young man with glasses studying a book. She gasped as it came to her that this must be the secretary. Then she thought she had to be wrong; that it was more probably some young graduate student doing research among her uncle's valuable books.

At any rate, she decided to find out who it was. She walked along the hall to the open doorway and knocked tentatively on the wooden door frame.

The young man looked up from his book; he had a fine-featured, intelligent face.

"Yes?" he said, rising.

"Are you Mr. Rand's secretary?" she asked.

He smiled. He had an interesting smile. "Yes," he said. "I suppose you could call me that. Actually, I'm his librarian."

"I'm his niece, Clare, I've just gotten in from Chicago," she said, entering the room and extending a hand to him.

"Of course," the young man said. "I'd forgotten. I just received this Byron first edition today, and I've been making a careful check of it. I'd forgotten everything else. I'm delighted to meet you. I understand you're going to be living with us. I'm Jeff Carney."

"This is very nice," she said, shaking hands.

He had dark hair, parted on the side, and sharp eyes that twinkled behind his horn-rimmed glasses. His suit was Ivy League, smartly cut, and he suggested more the alert college student than a dusty academic.

He asked, "Is this house new to you?"

"Yes. So is Boston."

"I think you'll like them both," the young man said.

She glanced around at the long narrow room, whose shelves were filled with books from floor to ceiling. There were desks and several chairs in the room, and files, paste pots, typewriters, magnifying glasses and other such items spread about. It was extremely impressive.

She said, "Are all these first editions?"

"A good many of them," he replied. "And we have a number of very valuable manuscripts including an illuminated Book of the Gospels which your uncle purchased in Spain a dozen years ago.

It was produced there by the monks in an abbey near Madrid. And the illumination was the work of a Sister Mary. She was a nun in a convent in Valencia. It's world-famous, valuable and the prize item of your uncle's collection. We keep all those things in the wall safe installed near my desk."

She looked and saw that there was indeed a wall safe under shelves of books in the area, at the end of the left wall. She said, "You're a regular librarian, then?"

He laughed. "Yes. I can prove it. I was with the Harvard Library for three years, then Boston University. And after that your uncle hired me."

"I imagine he needs someone with your knowledge," she said.

"He does, though he himself has a thorough knowledge of books himself. Though not a trained librarian, he is an excellent self-taught one. This was recognized by Virginia University, which has awarded him a doctorate in the field."

She raised her eyebrows. "I had no idea I had such an illustrious uncle."

"A very important man in his field," Jeff Carney assured her.

"I know nothing about rare books," she sighed. "Of course I like to read."

"You'll soon learn," the young man promised her. "I don't want to give anything away, but I know your uncle has plans for you."

"Really?"

"Yes. I think he wants me to train you as an assistant. There is a lot of routine work which takes my time. Although it is interesting, it slows me down in performing the important tasks."

Clare said, "I think I might enjoy it."

"I hope so," he said. "Please do sit down." He brought her out a chair with comfortable arms, and she sank into it. He shrugged, "Would you care for a liqueur?"

"That would be pleasant after dinner," she said. "I had my meal just before I left the plane."

"Any favorite?"

"Crème de cacao, if you have it," she said.

"I do," he assured her, and went across to a low chest which he opened to expose a well-stocked bar. He selected a bottle and glasses, poured the drinks on top of the chest, then brought them over on a tray. He passed hers to her and then sat down at his desk with his. The chair was swung so that he was facing her. "Welcome," he said.

"Thank you," she replied, taking a sip of the drink. "This is a lovely old house. So unique."

"It should be," he said. "It was designed by the noted American architect, Bulfinch. He did a number of houses in this area, the Statehouse and Massachusetts General Hospital among other things. Most of his buildings have come down in the last century, more's the pity, but there are still some like this left."

"Bulfinch dates back to the Revolutionary Period," she recalled. "This must be a truly old house!"

The young man offered her a mocking smile over his glass. "It is. Full of secret passages and ghosts!"

"Secret passages and ghosts!" she gasped.

He nodded. "In the old days, secret passages were standard items for mansions like this, as routine as plumbing today. They were times of violence, and the wealthy owners wanted a means of escape and a hiding place for valuables in the case of invasion or even merely robbers."

"I hadn't thought about that."

"It was very important in those days," he said.

"To the best of my knowledge, the secret passages are all sealed. But the ghost we do have."

"Truly?"

"Truly," he said, "though she doesn't go with this house. She's connected with one of the valuable books in Mr. Rand's collection. You will remember I spoke to you about his most prized possession being that Spanish Book of the Gospels, illuminated by Sister Mary of Valencia. Well, the Sister of Valencia is our ghost."

"Tell me about her," Clare begged, taking another sip of her drink.

He said, "People take the ghost very seriously. In fact that is how your uncle came by the manuscript. No one else at the time wanted to touch it."

"Why?"

"There is supposed to be a curse on the owner and his family."

"What sort of curse?"

"The legend goes that the Sister of Valencia went blind as a result of long years dedicating herself to the very fine color drawings or illuminations in the manuscript. And when she finished the task she asked her superiors that, as she'd given her eyes to God in the service of illustrating the manuscript, it should not leave religious hands. It should never be owned by anyone outside the church."

"But it has been, obviously, since my uncle now owns it."

"Times change and manuscripts are bartered," Jeff Carney said. "The Book of Gospels has had a half-dozen owners through the centuries. They all had one thing in common. Their lives were ended by violent tragedy, or someone dear to them died a mysterious death. And superstition has it that the deaths were due to the avenging Sister of

Valencia. She was angry that the book was taken from the monastery and so returned from the dead to destroy the various owners or those close to them."

Clare gave a tiny shudder. "It's not a pretty story."

"No," the young man said. "And the grim part of it is that your uncle has also had his share of ill fortune since he has owned the Book of Gospels. First, a villa he had rented in Spain burned down, and the manuscript was almost lost in the fire. Later, he moved to France, and thieves attempted to steal a number of his rare books, including the Book of Gospels. His secretary at that time was a young Frenchman. Your uncle always insists that a gun be kept ready in one of the library desks for such emergencies. The young man exchanged shots with the thieves and was killed."

"How awful!"

"Your uncle felt very badly. The young man's parents took it very hard. Your uncle invited them to call on him; the father came, but the mother refused to come. That was nine years ago, but your uncle has never forgotten it."

Clare said, "I'll ask the obvious question. Do you keep a gun here?"

"Yes." He smiled, patting the desk beside him. "In this desk. These days it would be foolish not to."

"I suppose you're right," she said. "But after that other awful experience, I would think my uncle wouldn't want to have weapons around. The books are insured, aren't they?"

"Yes," Jeff Carney said, "but it is more complicated than that. These volumes are for the most part unique. They can't be replaced. To a book lover like your uncle, no amount of money would make up for their loss."

"I can understand," she said.

"So you see the curse of the Sister of Valencia has been real enough for your uncle."

"What about her ghost?"

"It appears every so often," Jeff said. "I believe I have seen her once, though in these shadowy old halls and rooms you find it easy to imagine ghosts."

"I'd expect so," she agreed. "I must watch for her."

"She'll show herself to you soon enough," was the young man's warning. "She seems to take a special delight in terrifying newcomers."

"I'll remember that," she promised.

"Don't let me scare you," he hastened to say. "I only want to let you know what you might be exposed to. Most of the people in the house have had a brush with the good Sister."

"Then I'll surely see her," Clare said.

"I'd expect it," he said. "The legend associates her appearances with death for someone in the house. The last time I saw her, the charwoman who came here twice a week was run down by a car afterwards. Call it coincidence, but I've always felt strange about it."

"Have there been other instances like that?"

"I'm afraid so," the young man said. "But let's talk about more pleasant things. Your aunt and uncle are attending a Friends Of The Library meeting at Boston University. I don't expect them to be late. Their friend Professor Alan Curtis of Bedford University is with them. You'll be meeting him later. He's almost a constant visitor here."

She smiled wanly. "You've done a wonderful job filling me in on what life is like here."

Jeff put aside his glass. "It will take you time to learn that. You may find your uncle a little difficult, but he is basically a fine man, and his wife is also a talented person. She was secretary to the editor of the *Atlantic Monthly* a few years ago. And she is well-grounded in books."

"What sort of book collector would you say my uncle is?" she asked.

"A general collector. He has no particular area. From the time the Chinese invented printing in the Fifth Century, books have been printed, circulated and collected. Our culture being a trifle more backward, we first had printed works in the Fifteenth Century and from then on up to until today. In addition to museums, libraries and other institutions, there are thousands of private collectors."

"It has been Uncle Benjamin's main interest," she said.

"In all ages men have collected fine books," Jeff told her. "I'd say there are three general classes of book collectors: the bibliophile who tenderly loves a book for its own sake; the bibliomaniac, whose madness it is to possess certain books at all costs; and finally the bibliomoron, who deals in or owns rare books without knowing anything of their contents, the pleasures of handling them, or any of their fine points. Happily, your uncle belongs to group one."

"I'm glad you consider him a genuine lover of books," she said.

"He'll tell you about his collection later." Jeff smiled. "And perhaps you'll allow me to introduce you to Boston."

"That would be kind of you," she said.

"I'd enjoy it," the young man told her, turning to pick up the leather-bound volume of Byron he'd been studying before she arrived. "Books have great charm, but one does have to turn to human companions every so often."

"That sounds healthy," she said, amused.

"Living and working in a house this size sometimes tends to give one a touch of claustrophobia," he said. "It is a thing to be fought."

"I hope my arrival won't complicate things," she said.

"I see no reason it should," he told her. "Your Uncle Benjamin has been anxious about your arrival for some time. Perhaps I shouldn't say this, but he is concerned about the curse."

"Oh?"

"One night a few months ago, he saw the Sister of Valencia's phantom figure on the third landing when he was on his way up to his bedroom. It gave him a bad start."

"I should think so. Are you sure a shadow didn't cause his fright? What does this Sister of Valencia look like?"

"Like a nun of another era, in a gray robe with a cowl covering her head and her face overshadowed by it. No one ever sees the face. Usually they have a glimpse of the gray robe and perhaps the sight of a skeleton hand. As a rule they can't give much of a description afterward. They're too frightened."

'And Uncle Benjamin has seen the phantom?"

"Twice. The second occasion was only about two weeks ago. It has convinced him that he's marked for death, that the curse is going to destroy him. That is why he has been so anxious for you to get here. He wants to meet you and know you in case he might be struck down."

She gasped. "That's eerie!"

"Perhaps," Jeff said with a sigh. "But I'm afraid I must say the history of the Book of Gospels and its previous owners tends to make it seem that he's right."

CHAPTER TWO

Clare stared at the young man. "You're quite superstitious about it, then?"

"I suppose so," he admitted. "You know the legend, and then you see these things happen. It makes you wonder."

She frowned slightly. "If Uncle Benjamin is aware of the evil history of the Book of Gospels, why hasn't he sold it or given it to some museum?"

Jeff Carney smiled. "I think I explained it is the finest item in his collection. The idea of parting with it would be very painful to him. I believe he'd prefer to risk the curse and keep Sister Valencia's masterpiece."

As he finished talking, there was the sound of the front door opening downstairs and someone coming in. A man and a woman were chatting as they entered the lower hallway, and she guessed that her uncle and aunt had returned home.

Jeff confirmed this by rising and saying, "They've come back. I'll take you down to meet them."

She went downstairs with the young male secretary, feeling vaguely uneasy. It was difficult to tell how she would like these two whom she'd never met or how they'd react to her. By the time they reached the lower hall, Benjamin Rand and his wife Winifred had removed their coats and hats and placed them on the rack near the door. Now they turned to gaze at Clare with open interest.

Jeff went ahead and told her uncle, "This is your niece, Mr. Rand. She got here about an hour ago."

Uncle Benjamin came to Clare and took her by the hands; then he planted a paternal kiss on her cheek. He was a gray-haired man of medium size, with a pleasant face. His eyes were shrewd and his smile of greeting warm.

"My dear Clare," he said, "I'm delighted to have you here. Believe me, it is a moment I've looked forward to." He turned to the woman at his side. "And this is my wife, your Aunt Winifred."

Winifred Rand was younger in appearance than her husband. She had dark hair and wore glasses, which did not hide the intelligent, somewhat cold gleam in her eyes. She had the air of someone capable of organizing well, with a dislike for small talk or pretense. She dressed very smartly but in a subdued style and tended to be slightly overweight.

She came to Clare now, smiled and brushed her lips on the girl's cheek. "Welcome to Mount Vernon Street," she said in a voice which precisely matched her outward appearance.

"I hope I won't be a nuisance to you," Clare said.

"Not a chance!" her Uncle Benjamin told her. "We need someone young in the house. It is my hope you'll like the book field enough to want to work with Jeff here."

Jeff flashed her a smile. "I took the liberty of mentioning that," he said.

Uncle Benjamin gave him a look of mild interest as he drew his pipe from a side pocket of his jacket. "No harm done," he said. He told her, "We had to attend the meeting at the library. I was worried about your reception here, so I asked Jeff to work this evening."

"No problem," Jeff said. "I had plenty of work to catch up on."

Winifred Rand said, "There's no point in us standing here in the hall when we have a comfortable living room."

Uncle Benjamin nodded. "That is right. Let's go in and sit down. We have so much to talk about."

Clare entered the drawing room with her uncle. "All the rooms are so ornate," she said.

"It is a fine old house," he agreed. He pulled a high-backed chair toward a divan by the window and indicated she should sit in it. She did so, as he and his wife seated themselves on the divan.

In the doorway, Jeff Carney said, "If you people will excuse me, I'd like to finish working on the Byron book." He smiled at Clare. "I'll see you in the morning."

"Yes," she said, returning his smile. She'd liked the young librarian from the moment of their first meeting. And she was sure he discreetly wanted her to be alone with her newly discovered relatives.

Her Uncle Benjamin bade the young man good night. When he disappeared, her uncle turned to Clare and said, "I hardly dared hope for this moment. I was afraid you wouldn't leave Chicago and your friends there."

"It took some thinking about," she admitted.

"I'm sure it would," Winifred Rand agreed. "The prospect of coming here to live with older people who are almost strangers to you couldn't have been too appealing."

Benjamin Rand smiled at her, his pipe held in the corner of his mouth. "The thing is that you have come, and we're delighted to have you." He paused and sighed. "The misunderstanding between your father and myself should never have happened."

Clare wanted to spare him embarrassment, so she said, "I think we settled all that in our exchange of letters."

"True," her uncle said. "I'm glad you feel that way. So we'll get off to a fresh start?"

"I think that is the way it should be," she agreed.

Winifred Rand said, "I hope you like your room."

"It's very nice," she said.

Benjamin Rand sighed. "I'm glad you think so. There are some things about the house that are not so charming. But there is plenty of time to talk about such things. You must be tired from your journey."

"I am, a little," she said. "If you don't mind, I think I may go to bed early."

Winifred Rand got to her feet. "You should. You look tired, and you'll have a lot of adjustments to make in the days ahead."

"Exactly," her uncle said, rising and taking his pipe from his mouth. "The thing we want you to remember is that we are chiefly interested in your being happy here."

"I'd say you've done everything possible to insure that," Clare told them.

Good nights were exchanged, and she went up the several flights of stairs to her fourth floor bedroom. She'd been conscious that her uncle and aunt had been studying her intently, sizing her up, deciding what sort of person she was. And while she didn't resent this, it had made her slightly uneasy. She could only hope she'd made a good impression on them.

She switched on the light in her bedroom and went over to the dresser, preparatory to retiring for the night. Staring at her reflection in the dresser mirror, she began removing her earrings and then took off a gold chain necklace which she'd worn to set off her plain green traveling dress. She left the earrings and necklace on the dresser top rather than bothering to place them in the cases in which they were usually kept. She was tired, and there would be plenty of time to take care of them later.

The set of earrings and necklace had been inherited from her mother and were the best pieces of jewelry she owned. The rich gold always had the effect of making a plain dress look better, which was why she'd chosen to wear the set. The house was very silent, and she guessed that Jeff Carney might already have come up to bed. There had been no lights on in the library when she went by it.

Finally she slipped into bed and turned out the lights.

It was not strange that she should dream during the night and that her dream should include handsome Jeff Carney and the ghost. She dreamed that the young man had taken her up onto the roof top to enjoy the view of Boston. Then he had been called away on some errand and had left her alone there for a while. While she was gazing over the brick parapet, she'd gradually become aware of another presence on the roof. The realization of this had sent a chill through her. Then she turned and, standing there behind her, was a weird-looking figure in a gray habit and cowl which hid the face.

It took her only a second to decide who it was. The avenging Nun of Valencia! The ghost of the nun who had become blind as a result of her dedicated efforts illuminating the pages of the Book of Gospels in long-ago Spain. The phantom reached out a hand toward her, and she saw that the hand was a skeleton hand, bones without flesh! She let out a cry of fear and edged along the roof top in an effort to get to the door leading down into the building and her route to escape.

But the gray menace of the Nun of Valencia followed her and kept between her and the door. Gradually the phantom moved nearer to her, until at last one of the bony hands reached out and grasped her by the wrist! She screamed, and as she screamed the scene changed, and she was in a dark cave. She was alone and running from something, something which threatened her. She halted, listened and heard footsteps in the dark passage behind her rapidly gaining on her. She cried out in fear, and her cries echoed in the weird cavern.

The scene changed again. She was in the library, and her Uncle Benjamin had his back to her as he removed a book from one of the many filled shelves. He turned to her with a serious look and opened the book. There, writhing between its pages, was a tiny, gray-speckled, writhing adder. She drew back in horror! Her dreams became confused after that, and there was no pattern to them, except that she had the feeling she was fleeing from some unknown danger.

She awoke, and it was morning, a rather gray autumn morning. Raising herself on an elbow, she thought about her dreams and wondered what they had meant.

Getting up, she washed and dressed and put on a plain print dress which she deemed suitable for her first day there. She was about to go down to breakfast when she decided to put away in the proper cases, the jewelry she'd worn the night before. Producing the cases from one of her partially unpacked bags, she went to the dresser to find the earrings and necklace. They weren't there!

She couldn't believe it! She distinctly recalled taking them off and placing them on the dresser top, and now they were gone! Had some thief entered her room during the night? There was no lock or bolt on her bedroom door, and so this could be possible. But she doubted that there would be any thief in her uncle's house. Yet her jewelry had vanished!

Standing there in bewilderment, she tried to decide what to do. To go down to breakfast with a story like this would not be the ideal way to begin her stay with her uncle and aunt. But there was nothing else she could do. She crossed the room to leave the jewelry cases in the bag when her eyes caught a gleam on a table by the window. There on this table were her earrings and necklace!

Clare crossed to the table and picked them up with an expression of astonishment on her attractive face. It was almost too much! She was so very certain she'd left the jewelry on her dresser, and in some mysterious fashion it had been moved to another area of the room. How? By human hands, or had some phantom presence transferred them? Either way, it made for an unpleasant mystery!

After a moment she put the gold jewelry pieces in their cases and locked them in her suitcase. Then she went down to the ground floor and discovered her Aunt Winifred to be the only one at the breakfast table. The rather cold woman greeted her with a thin smile.

"Did you rest well?" the older woman asked.

"I slept quite soundly, considering that the bed and surroundings were new," Clare said as she sat down.

"There is no noise on this street after midnight," Winifred Rand said. "And our bedrooms are mostly at the rear of the house."

"I gathered that," Clare said.

Aunt Winifred gave her a searching glance. "Do you think you'll be happy here?"

The question surprised Clare a little. She said, "I hope so. I hardly know yet. I've been here such a short time." She helped herself to orange juice, which had been set out for her.

The dark woman looked grim. "I'd understand if you didn't share your uncle's enthusiasm for books and this rather menacing old house. The atmosphere occasionally bothers me."

Clare said, "I think the books are fascinating, although I know little about them."

"I trust you'll still think so when you become more familiar with the history of the library," was Winifred Rand's comment. "It has an unhappy history."

"In what way?" Clare asked, reaching for the toast.

The older woman said, "A young man lost his life trying to keep some of Benjamin's valuable books from being stolen. This happened in France some time ago. Your uncle didn't seem to mind as long as his precious books weren't taken. But I was shocked by the tragedy, and I don't think I've ever felt the same about the collection since."

"It must have been a dreadful experience to go through," Clare said.

"Many of the ancient volumes in the library have a violent history," her uncle's wife went on. "They have been rescued from fire in some city pillaged by invading troops, or they were the property of some well-known personage who came to a tragic end, or they have some ghostly legend attached to them, as the Book of Gospels does."

"They are bound to have a history," Clare agreed.

Winifred looked grim. "And such grisly histories," she said. "I often think they cast a pall of bad luck over the house. But Benjamin refuses to admit anything like that. To him a book is a prized possession, and he doesn't think beyond that."

"Perhaps it's just as well," Clare suggested.

"Perhaps," the older woman said doubtfully. "For my own part, I wish Benjamin would give up his collecting. He's dedicated his life to it, and Bedford University is anxious to take over the library at his death. I say to donate it to them now, and let them have the responsibility, while we enjoy our few remaining years without a lot of headaches."

"You're not that old," Clare chided her. "You both seem younger than I expected."

"We aren't that young," Winifred Rand assured her in her prim fashion. "I'm glad you've come. Benjamin was very worried about you. Of course, I'm not sure whether being here is the best thing for you or not."

Clare said, "Uncle Benjamin and you are my only two close relatives living in the East. I've lost contact with Mother since her marriage."

"She does write you?"

"Occasionally. But neither of us is a good correspondent."

Her aunt regarded her bleakly. "Your Uncle

Benjamin is very anxious to make up to you for his quarrel with your father. And he plans to be most generous."

"There is no need," Clare protested, feeling embarrassed.

"I have told him the same thing," her aunt said. "It is my belief that inherited money does little for people. Better to make it on your own."

"I have come here chiefly to get to know you and Uncle Benjamin," she said. "I had no thought of inheritance in mind, and I don't expect any."

Winifred sat back from the table with a sigh. "Well, if I were in your place, I wouldn't refuse anything. But on the other hand, I can't see that any prospect of an inheritance would repay you for living an unhappy existence here."

"If I find I'm unhappy here, I'll surely leave," she said, a little surprised that her aunt should emphasize this point so.

"I think that would be smart on your part," Winifred said. "Jeff Carney is about your age. Having him in the house should help. He's a nice young man, but, like Benjamin, his first interest is the library."

Clare managed a smile. "It is his career."

"True," Winifred said. "Benjamin has a very strong sense of family. The quarrel with your father upset him greatly. I'm not like that. I have seen little of my remaining family for years."

"But you do have some relatives?"

"Yes," Winifred Rand said, rising. "I can't think what Benjamin would say if I brought a distant cousin into the house. He'd feel it an intrusion. Yet he expects me to accept you without any question."

Clare felt her cheeks warm. "I hope I won't be a bother to you."

"You won't," the dark woman with the glasses assured her. "I'm merely trying to make you understand how my husband's mind works. He can be extremely selfish in some things."

"I suppose that is true of most of us," Clare said.

"In some cases, it is more marked than in others," Winifred Rand said. And with that she left the room.

Clare finished her breakfast alone. It seemed to her she had heard the first rumbling of annoyance from her Aunt Winifred. And she worried that this might be only a beginning. It was apparent that the older woman resented her.

Breakfast over, she went upstairs to the library and found Jeff Carney there. He was wearing dark gray trousers and a gray jacket with black leather patches on the elbows.

He rose from his desk as she came into the room. "It's a gray morning for your first day in Boston," he said. "Accept my apologies."

"I really hadn't noticed. Everything here is so new."

"Your uncle has gone to Lauriat's to attend a book auction of an estate in Andover," Jeff said. "He should be back fairly early, surely in time for lunch."

Clare indicated the desk. "Do you work here day after day?"

"I get out occasionally," he said, the eyes behind the glasses twinkling. "I go to the Public Library for information, and to the bank to look after the business details of running the collection."

"I'm glad," she said. "I imagine it would be very confining otherwise."

He said, "If you take over part of my chores, I

may not get out so much. I must be careful about that."

Clare smiled. "I don't imagine my uncle will trust me with any important errands for a while." She went over to the desk where he'd been working. "What volume is getting your attention this morning?"

He said, "It's interesting, though not actually valuable. 'The Writings of John Bouroughs'; published here in Boston about the turn of the century. It's one of twenty-two volumes of an autographed edition of seven hundred and fifty. The binding is good, morocco-tooled."

"I can see that I have a lot to learn," she said.

"It's a tremendous field," he agreed. "But then your uncle only deals in one area of it. And this is a modest collection by some standards, though large for a private collector."

"Aunt Winifred mentioned that Bedford University is anxious to take over the collection, and she would like to have Uncle agree."

Jeff nodded. "Professor Alan Curtis keeps talking to your uncle about it, but he hasn't gotten any agreement from him as yet."

Clare looked at the young man. "Do you think it would be a good idea for him to sell his collection?"

Jeff shrugged. "It would make him wealthier, but I doubt if he'd be happier. Of course he'd have much less responsibility and more time to enjoy himself doing other things, if he would enjoy that."

She said, "You sound as if you think he wouldn't."

"I guess that's my opinion," the young man said. "In any case, Professor Curtis is hoping your uncle will either give his books to Bedford University while he's alive or will them to him when he's dead, so I doubt whether there would be any money involved. There wouldn't have to be. Your uncle is a very wealthy man."

Clare said thoughtfully, "Then my aunt's reasons must have to do with the excessive time he gives to the collection and his tragic experiences as a collector. She mentioned that young man being killed. And though she didn't mention the ghost I'm sure it must worry her."

"Winifred is troubled by the Nun of Valencia," Jeff agreed. "I think that may be her chief reason for wishing your uncle to abandon the collection."

Clare gave him a knowing glance. "I had some bad dreams last night. I blame them on you and your ghost stories."

"Sorry," he said. "That wasn't my intention."

"I'm sure of that. But still, you did make me realize there's a strange atmosphere about this old place. Aunt Winifred blames it on the books and the weight of their combined histories."

"It's an imaginative approach."

Her eyes met his. "Something else happened which puzzled me."

"What?"

"It concerns the jewelry I was wearing last night," she said. And she went on to tell him about the incident.

Jeff's face clouded. "That's not as unusual as you may think," he told her. "Things of that sort have happened here before."

"What does it mean?"

"It's typical," the young librarian said earnestly. "The chances are that the phantom paid a call on you last night."

CHAPTER THREE

"The Nun of Valencia," she gasped.

Jeff nodded. "We've had things moved about here in the library. There's been absolutely no other explanation for the happenings. We have had to blame the ghost."

"That gives me a nice uneasy feeling," she said wryly. "And it had to happen on my first night here."

"I warned you she generally had a special greeting for newcomers."

"So you did," she remembered.

"But I wouldn't let it frighten you away," the young man went on. "I doubt if she'll try to harm you. If there's anyone in danger in this house, it's your uncle."

"I am his blood relative," Clare reminded him. "Perhaps the ghost wants to strike at him through me."

Jeff shook his head. "I'd expect any misfortune to happen to your uncle first. But I don't have the fear of the ghost that he has."

"Yet you believe in it."

"I have to accept the evidence of my eyes. I've seen it briefly several times."

"This is a strange situation," she marveled. "I had no idea I'd be finding myself in a haunted house."

He smiled. "So many of these old mansions have a ghost that it oughtn't to surprise you."

"I've heard stories," she said. "But I've never put much stock in them."

"This gives you an actual experience," Jeff said. "But if I were you, I'd try to ignore what happened. You're going to have some other exciting experiences here of a different nature. Later on, your uncle will show you the Book of Gospels and the copy of the Gutenberg Bible he owns."

She was impressed. "Does he actually have a Gutenberg Bible?"

"Yes. He purchased it since I've been with him. It cost him high in six figures. You'll admire its rich, solemn Gothic letters. Its beauty can be appreciated by anyone."

"Is there anything I can do?" she asked.

Jeff smiled. "Are you so anxious to begin work?"

"Yes. You have me interested," she said.

"Very well," the young man told her. "We've just bought a set of the novels of Samuel Richardson. There are twenty volumes, and you can go through them and check for any missing pages or any notes or signatures that may be found in them." He led her over to a desk almost directly opposite his, where the pile of cloth-bound books awaited her.

She sat down to go through the books with a pencil and a writing pad to make notations. From her desk she had a view of the opposite side of the street. Every so often she paused to watch the passing traffic and pedestrians. The time passed quickly, and she found only one volume of the set which was damaged. There were about thirty pages missing. She made a note of this along with some other entries concerning dates and signatures marked on the flyleaf of several of the volumes.

Her Uncle Benjamin did not return for lunch. He phoned to say that he'd met a fellow collector at the book auction and that they were having luncheon together at his club. Jeff informed her that he had had only a glass of milk for lunch but that Mrs. Fox would get her any kind of light snack. She decided on a cheese sandwich and milk, which she had in the library with him.

Her Aunt Winifred had gone out on either a shopping or visiting expedition, so they were alone in the house except for Mrs. Fox. Clare enjoyed the quiet and easy working pace after the rigors of her job in Chicago. She didn't know how long the new atmosphere would continue to appeal to her, but thus far she'd found it enjoyable.

As she and Jeff sat finishing their glasses of milk, she said, "I suspect that Aunt Winifred is not too happy about my coming here."

"You think not?"

"I'm almost sure of it," she said. "We talked at breakfast, and she pointed out that Uncle Benjamin wouldn't tolerate any of her relatives here, but that he expected her to welcome me."

Jeff's eyebrows raised. "That was putting it plainly enough."

"I thought so," she said.

"She's a rather strange person," Jeff warned her. "I don't know why she married your uncle. They haven't that much in common. I suspect she was interested in his money. Maybe she sees you as a threat to siphon some of it off."

"There's no doubt of it."

"I'd stand up to her. Your uncle often has to. They get along only because he treats her firmly."

Clare smiled forlornly. "That isn't quite so easy for me."

"Still, you musn't give in. You owe that to your uncle. In many ways he's a very lonely man. He needs you."

"I'd like to believe that," she said.

"You can."

They went back to work. He continued with the volumes of Byron, while she moved on to a four-volume set of Samuel Pepys' *Diary and Correspondence.* She forgot that she was editing a rare edition and began reading it for sheer enjoyment. She was lost in the quaint account of his romantic adventures in his wife's absence when the doorbell rang. Mrs. Fox answered it and ushered in a man who spoke in a friendly, casual fashion and who had a hint of a British accent.

Jeff got up at once. "That will be Professor Alan Curtis of Bedford University," he told her.

"The one who hopes to get the collection?" she said.

"Yes. He's a close friend of your Uncle Benjamin's. He comes here often."

As the young man finished speaking, Professor Curtis entered the library. He was a man of medium height and weight, with a round, good-natured face, shrewd brown eyes and curly brown hair parted in the middle. He was dressed in a smartly tailored gray suit and was wearing a light trench coat.

"Good afternoon," he said warmly, beaming at her. "I take it this is the niece from Chicago. I'm delighted to meet you. I'm Alan Curtis."

She shook hands with him. "And I've heard a good deal about you, Professor Curtis."

He waved an impatient hand. "Do call me Alan! I'm a familiar in this house." He gave Jeff a humorous glance. "That doesn't sound indecent, does it?"

"Not noticeably," Jeff said, laughing.

"Where is Benjamin?" the professor wanted to know.

"He attended a book auction at Lauriat's, and now he's spending some time with another collector. They're having lunch together," Jeff said.

"Now I call that a true waste of time," Professor Curtis said. "I wanted him to meet me and go to the university to check on a list of offerings from London. He told me he'd be here."

Jeff said, "He must have forgotten."

"Indeed he must have," the professor said. He turned his attention to Clare. "And I see they have you profitably employed. Isn't Pepys a delight?"

"He is," she agreed enthusiastically. "I've been reading rather than checking the condition of the volumes as I'm supposed to be doing."

Professor Curtis smiled at her. "And so to bed! One of my boyhood pleasures was devouring Pepys." He turned to Alan. "Has she seen the treasures of her uncle's book collection?"

"Not yet," Jeff said. "She only arrived last night, and Mr. Rand has been out all day."

"Most thoughtless of him, since he was supposed to be here when I arrived," the professor said. Turning to her, he added, "Wait until you see the gems of your uncle's collection. He keeps promising me the university will get them, but he never makes a move to give them to me. He apparently enjoys my torment of waiting."

She smiled. "If he has promised them to you, no doubt you'll get them some day."

"Some day is so indefinite." The rotund professor sighed. "There is only one volume I do not want. That is the illuminated manuscript, the Book of Gospels! You've heard about the ghost?"

"Yes," she said.

Professor Curtis grimaced. "I refuse to be stalked through the university corridors by the Nun of Valencia. That gray-clad phantom is not my idea of merry company. You know she tries to wreak her vengeance on anyone who takes over the manuscript and keeps it from being returned to the church."

"I've heard the legend," she said.

The professor gave her a warning look. "I do not regard it as a legend. I call it solid fact. That phantom has made a number of appearances under this roof."

"So I've been told," she said.

"You have been told truly," the professor assured her. "Be cautious while you are here. That is my warning to you."

Jeff interposed, "You're trying to frighten her."

"Facts, my dear fellow," Professor Alan Curtis said. "I deal only in facts. The Nun of Valencia exists. There is solid evidence of it."

Jeff seemed anxious to distract the professor from his ghost talk. He said, "Have you any message you want me to give Mr. Rand?"

"Tell him he has disappointed me," the professor said, "and that I shall expect him to come by the university tomorrow about ten to go over that London listing with me. I want to cable some immediate offers for any books he recommends."

"I'll give him the message," Jeff promised.

Professor Alan Curtis beamed at her again. "A true pleasure meeting you, Clare. I trust we may meet soon again and frequently. And remember what I've told you about the avenging nun."

"I'm not liable to forget," she said.

"Forewarned is forearmed," the professor said earnestly. Then he bade them goodbye. Jeff saw him to the door, and she went back to her desk and Samuel Pepys' journals. She was getting down to work when Jeff returned.

The young librarian's eyes twinkled behind his glasses. "You made a conquest of Professor Curtis. He feels you're a charming addition to the household."

"How nice," she said. And they both settled down to work once more.

When they finished for the day, Jeff invited her to attend a musical revue at the Somerset Hotel with him. She accepted and arranged to meet him at eight o'clock, as they would need a half-hour to get to the hotel.

Jeff said, "You'll be having dinner with your aunt and uncle?"

"I suppose so."

"They never eat their evening meal at home, you know."

"They don't?"

"No. They go to Pierre's. It's a nice little French restaurant next door. It's owned by a Pierre Reaux and his wife. Pierre is the headwaiter, and his wife is the chef. They came here directly from France and bought the building next to this one. The restaurant is on the ground floor, and they rent apartments in the basement and on the floors above. All in all, they make a good living."

Clare was surprised. "And you say they have their dinner there every night?"

"Unless they are out of town or invited out somewhere," the librarian said.

"I should think they'd get tired of it."

"Madame Reaux is a good cook, and she varies

the menus. I hear she also makes her husband toe the line. She gives all the orders. He is her second husband, and it was her money that bought the building and started the restaurant."

Clare smiled. "She sounds like a large, overwhelming person."

"No," he said. "You see her only rarely. She is a thin woman of middle age with a mild manner. Not the type you'd expect at all."

Clare went upstairs and showered and changed into a dress suitable for the evening. She had no sooner gotten ready than there was a knock on her door.

She opened it to discover her Uncle Benjamin. She said, "I wondered if you'd gotten home."

"A short while ago," Uncle Benjamin said. "Are you ready to have dinner?"

"Yes. I'm meeting Jeff at eight to attend a show."

"Then we should go to dinner at once," her uncle said. A small cloud crossed his pleasant face. "Your Aunt Winifred has a headache, so she will not be joining us at dinner. But I'm all ready to go."

Clare said, "I hope Aunt Winifred isn't really ill."

"No, just a slight indisposition. She has these headaches now and then. Nothing to worry about," her uncle said.

She went downstairs with him, and they went outside and down the front steps, walked up the hill to the next house and mounted its steps to enter Pierre's restaurant. It was a small, rather charming place, with paneled wood walls and a few appropriate paintings to set the mood. There were some booths and tables. Since there were just two of them, her Uncle Benjamin selected a suitably remote booth. He ordered, and they began to talk as they waited to be served.

Uncle Benjamin told her, "You mustn't mind if Winifred behaves in a hostile way. She resents my having you in the house."

"I was worried about that," Clare said.

"Don't let it trouble you," her Uncle Benjamin told her. "I want you with me, and she is not going to change things."

"I don't want to cause trouble."

"She'll give up her sullen spells when she finds they aren't getting her anywhere," her uncle assured her. "I've been through this with her before."

"If I stay, I'll do so only because you insist on it," she said.

"I do. You're here, and here you'll remain. I have writen you into my will, and I want to know you better in case anything should happen to me."

She frowned. "What do you fear might happen?"

"I may be murdered," he said calmly.

"Murdered!" she gasped.

"Yes," he said, his sharp eyes studying her. "You have heard about the Nun of Valencia."

"I have. But do you seriously think there is such a phantom and that she might try to kill you?"

"I'm positive of it," he said solemnly. "I've seen it. So have my wife and Jeff. You can ask them."

"But why should the ghost single you out?"

"Because I'm the present owner of the Book of Gospels, the manuscript she illuminated."

"I've heard about that. She went blind after she completed the task, didn't she?"

"Yes. And she made the religious order holding the manuscript promise it would never leave church hands. Of course it has."

"If you truly believe in the legend, you should give the manuscript to Bedford University," she said.

"I will when I'm done with it. But not yet."

"You prefer to risk death rather than give it up?"

He smiled bleakly. "A collector will pay almost any price for his obsession."

"I hope your fears are groundless," she said.

"So do I." Her uncle sighed. "But I have good reasons to believe that they are not."

Their dinner arrived, and Pierre Reaux came personally to see if it was satisfactory. When everything had been checked and found to be satisfactory, he vanished. The food was excellent, and Clare forgot her worries and tensions regarding the old mansion for a while.

As they left the restaurant, a thin, sad-eyed woman with blonde hair turned almost gray greeted them from behind the cash register. She spoke a greeting to her Uncle Benjamin in French, and he introduced her to Clare. It developed that she was the Madame Reaux who ruled her husband and the restaurant with an iron hand. She gave Clare a thin smile.

"A strange person," Clare said as they walked down the steps of the restaurant to hilly Mount Vernon Street.

"Interested only in her kitchen," her Uncle Benjamin said. "You seldom see her in the restaurant. Tonight was an exception."

They returned to her uncle's house, where Jeff was already downstairs waiting for Clare. She thanked her uncle for the dinner and then rushed upstairs to get her coat.

Jeff had a taxi waiting when she returned downstairs. They were driven to the Somerset Hotel and went in to the room which was being used as a musical theatre. It was intimate, and Jeff had ringside tickets. There was a fairly good crowd in attendance, and the performers were young but competent. Clare enjoyed the show. When they left the hotel, they strolled a little before hailing another taxi.

Jeff said, "Tonight was fun."

"It was for me," Clare said happily.

"We must do something like it again," he said.

"I'd enjoy it."

"There are plenty of things to see and do in Boston," he told her.

She smiled up at him as they strolled along the wide pavement with neon-lighted buildings in the distance. It was cool but pleasant.

"One of the nice things about being on Mount Vernon Street has been getting to know you," she said.

Jeff gazed down at her fondly. "And having you around is a big plus for me. I had thought about leaving your uncle. Now I'm glad I didn't."

She gave him an urgent look. "You mustn't do that. I'm sure he needs you badly."

"I won't go now," Jeff said.

They found a taxi, and on the drive back he placed an arm around her. And when he escorted her into the silent house on Mount Vernon Street, he kissed her good night.

When they reached the fourth floor, he went on down the long corridor toward the rear of the house, and she entered her own room. She closed the door behind her with a dreamy smile on her lovely face. It had been a good evening.

She quickly undressed and got into bed. She fell

asleep almost as soon as she turned out the light. Her sleep was dreamless, and she had no idea how long she slept. She awoke with a start to find the room was still in darkness and someone was knocking gently on her door.

She sat up in bed with a troubled expression on her face. Then she called out, "Yes?"

The light knocking came again.

Thoroughly awake now, she swung out of bed and put on her slippers. Then she crossed the darkness of the room to the door. She put her ear to it.

"Who is it?" she asked.

"Clare!" Her name was whispered urgently.

"Yes?"

"Clare!" The same urgent whisper again.

The door was not locked. An intruder could easily enter. Yet Clare was unwilling to cooperate by opening the door until she had some idea who was out there.

Still with her ear close to the door, she demanded, "Who is there?"

"Clare!" the whisper came once more.

She began to speculate on who it might be. Perhaps her Uncle Benjamin or Jeff. It might even be her Aunt Winifred. She debated as to what she should do and finally decided she might as well open the door.

She did and stared into the hallway. It was dark, and there was no one in sight. She hesitated and then took a step out of the room so that she was standing directly in the dark hall. She was astonished that she could neither hear nor see anyone. Had whoever it was become tired of waiting and left?

She was about to go back into her room when she heard a soft cough from down the corridor near the head of the stairs. It came for only a moment, and then there was that strange silence again. She began to feel nervous. And she again debated as to whether she should return to her room or not. But her curiosity had been aroused, and she was also worried that she might be needed.

Slowly she advanced down the dark hall, a chill descending her spine. Her frightened eyes sought the shadows for some hint of a figure, but there was none. She moved hesitantly, not knowing when she might encounter the mysterious being who had whispered her name so frantically. What had it meant?

She reached the head of the stairs, whence the cough had seemed to come, and stood there, her whole body taut. She clasped the railing and gazed around her into the shadows apprehensively. But still she could see nothing.

Then from below came the same eerie whisper: "Clare!"

She stiffened and, still clutching the rail, called back in a low voice, "Yes?"

"Clare!"

The whisper had almost a hypnotic quality to it. Discretion should have warned her to go back to her room while she was still safe. But curiosity, combined with the weird attraction the whisper seemed to have for her, drove her on. Very slowly she began to descend the stairway.

The last whisper had come from the landing of the floor where her uncle and aunt had their bedroom. She was beginning to think it must have been one or the other of them. At last she reached the third floor, and it was as dark as the one above. She stood there hesitantly.

Then from behind her there came a rustling sound. In the next moment something struck her from the darkness and sent her pitching headlong down the stairs with a frantic scream!

CHAPTER FOUR

Clare had blacked out. Now she stirred and opened her eyes to look up into the stern face of Winifred Rand. The big woman had a nightcap on over hair rolled in curlers and was wearing a dressing gown. She was on her knees beside Clare on the second landing just beyond the library entrance. A light had been turned on so Clare could see everything clearly.

"What happened to you?" Winifred Rand demanded. "Are you prone to walking in your sleep?"

"No," Clare said weakly, raising herself upon an elbow. "Someone came to my door and whispered my name. I followed the voice down to your floor, and then someone came up behind me in the darkness and shoved me down the stairs!"

The older woman frowned at her. "That's quite a story!"

"It's true," Clare said, gradually regaining some poise. She had a bruised arm and hip, but she didn't think any bones had been broken. "I could have been badly hurt."

"You were on the floor here in a faint when I came to you," Winifred said.

"Where is Uncle Benjamin? Why isn't he here? Surely he must have heard me fall if you did!"

The older woman regarded her calmly. "Your uncle takes sleeping tablets every night. He didn't hear you."

Clare struggled to her feet. "Surely Jeff or Mrs. Fox ought to have been able to hear my scream!"

"Mrs. Fox is in a room at the back next to the kitchen," Winifred explained patiently. "And Jeff's room is also at the very back of the house. I doubt if either of them could have heard you. My room is at the head of the stairway, so I couldn't escape hearing you."

Clare gave the older woman a suspicious glance. She was already beginning to suspect that it had been Winifred who had lured her out to the hallway and down the steps, then pushed her in an effort to frighten her away from the old mansion.

She said, "Did you see anyone when you came out to help me?"

"No," Winifred said stoically. "And I switched on the lights as soon as I came into the hall. I saw you in a crumpled heap down here, but no one else."

"There had to be someone!"

Winifred eyed her with cold arrogance. "Why do you say that?"

"I was shoved down the stairs!"

"Couldn't you have stumbled? Lost your footing in the darkness?"

"No. I felt hands or something come up behind me and catch me by the shoulder blades. It was a tremendous force, enough to send me plunging down here!"

The older woman looked unimpressed. "It all must have taken place very swiftly."

"It did!"

"And don't you think you may have imagined some of it?"

"No," Claire said, distraught that the woman should doubt her word. "You saw me down here!"

"Yes. And my first thought was that you'd stumbled in the dark. Other people have, on those stairs."

"That wasn't so in my case," Clare argued.

Winifred said slowly, "Then you're saying that someone attacked you with intent to maim or kill?"

"I am!"

"That's a strong charge," the older woman warned her. "Who could have done such a thing?"

"I don't know."

"That isn't very helpful," Winifred said. "To prove there was an attack on you, it will be necessary to find some person with sufficient motive."

Clare had it on the tip of her tongue to accuse the older woman. But she fought the impulse and contented herself with, "I think we might find someone."

The older woman shrugged. "I'd say you were lucky to escape serious injury, and I suspect you've been the victim of a nightmare. The best thing you can do is go back to bed before we wake up the others."

Clare showed distress. "Shouldn't we wake one of them and have them search for a clue that there was someone in here?"

"No," Winifred said. "I will not wake my husband or Jeff Carney."

Clare stared at the older woman's stern face. "In that case, you're saying that my testimony counts for nothing, that it was all a product of my imagination."

Winifred sighed. "Yes. That describes my reactions fairly well."

Clare was shocked. "I see."

"So let us return to our rooms," the older woman suggested.

"Very well," Clare said grimly. She was now convinced that Winifred had played the eerie trick on her and tried to kill her by shoving her downstairs. But there would be little chance of proving this either to her uncle or Jeff. Not having been on the scene, they wouldn't understand.

At the third landing, Winifred said, "I hope your sleep is not disturbed again. If you should hear other whispers from the hallway, I'd ignore them."

"No need to warn me about that," Clare said worriedly. She left the older woman, went on up to the fourth floor and started down the dark hallway to her bedroom.

She'd gone only a few steps when she saw a shadowy figure at the end of the hall. She stopped, filled with new fears, and watched as the figure drew nearer. Then she saw that it was Jeff, in dressing gown and pajamas, and she drew a deep sigh of relief.

Jeff came to her. "What's going on?"

"I've had a strange experience," she told him.

"Tell me about it," he said as they stood facing each other in the near-darkness of the hall.

She did, ending with, "I left Winifred just now."

The young librarian frowned. "Something weird is going on here. And Mrs. Fox was up. I saw her on the rear stairway just as I left my room. I assumed she had heard the noise and was on her way to see what was wrong."

"She didn't arrive until after we started upstairs," Clare said.

Jeff gave her a knowing look. "That brings up a new possibility. Could it have been Mrs. Fox who enticed you into the hall and then shoved you down the stairs?"

"It could have been. I can't think of any motive she would have, though she's not been friendly to me since I arrived."

"She might be acting for someone else with a sufficient motive to want to be rid of you."

"You mean Winifred?"

"Possibly," the young man said.

"I've thought of that," Clare agreed. "I even wondered if it wasn't Winifred herself who attacked me."

"We've left out another interesting possibility," Jeff told her.

"Oh?"

"The ghost," he said. "The Nun of Valencia!"

She stared up at his handsome face through the shadows. "Do you honestly consider her a suspect?"

"I must, since I admit her existence," Jeff said.

Clare sighed. "Then that leaves us absolutely nowhere!"

"I wouldn't say that."

"I would," she said. "I'm terrified of this house now. What am I to do?"

The young man said, "You're not thinking of leaving."

"I could have been badly hurt tonight, perhaps killed!"

"Don't be scared off so easily," Jeff begged her. "Stay and see the thing through. Your uncle needs you."

She looked at him solemnly. "And someone is very anxious to make me leave."

"I won't deny that. You'll have to be more careful in the future."

"If it's a ghost I'm dealing with, and you say that is possible, I can't imagine carefulness making much difference."

Jeff said, "You'll feel differently about it in the morning. Just wait and see."

"I will." She sighed. "But I'm sure I won't sleep any more tonight."

"Try," he said. "Leave the lights on in your room."

"Then I'd never sleep. I'll have to brave the dark and trust that sleep comes."

"I'm not all that far away," Jeff reminded her. "If you have any further trouble, scream. I'll be bound to hear you and come."

"I'll depend on that," she told him.

Jeff accompanied her to her door and saw her in safely. She closed the door and went over to her bed. Somehow it seemed unlikely that the ghost would return again that night. She slipped between the sheets and turned out the light on her bedside table. Then, staring into the darkness, she tried to court sleep and finally succeeded.

When she awakened it was morning, and a sunny day this time. The bruise marks on her arm and hip showed clearly. They were reminders of the ordeal of the previous night. She got up and dressed, being careful to notice if the order of anything had been changed in her room. She found no changes.

The dining room was empty when she went downstairs. Mrs. Fox left a buffet breakfast on the table so that they could help themselves. The coffeepot was plugged in and ready to be used.

She served herself orange juice, toast and coffee as she speculated on where Winifred and the housekeeper could be. Perhaps they felt guilty and were deliberately keeping out of the way.

When she finished breakfast, she went up to the library. She found her Uncle Benjamin high on a ladder, removing books from an upper shelf. Seeing her, he came down with a book under his arm. "Do you have any plans for the day?" he wanted to know.

"You can help me with these," her Uncle Benjamin said with one of his shy smiles. It was evident that no one had told him of her accident of the night before. And she decided that, for the moment at least, there would be no point in burdening him with it.

She asked, "What are they?"

"Rudyard Kipling," he said. "It's a thirty-two volume set published in New York in 1899. The binding is leather and gold. Each of the volumes has been signed by the author. The set is worth a good price. I need to dust the volumes and see they are in good shape. Then I'll return them up there again."

Clare smiled at him. "The library is your life, isn't it?"

"Very much so," he said.

"Where is Jeff?"

"Out to the bank," her uncle said. "He does most of my banking for me. He's extremely competent."

"I'm sure of that," she said.

Uncle Benjamin put aside the book he was holding. He said, "While I think of it, let me show you some of the real treasures of my collection."

She went down to the end of the room with him as he knelt on the carpet and, with a slight frown on his face, began to twirl the controls of the old-fashioned safe built to fit in flush with the bookcases.

After a few moments he gave a satisfied sigh and swung the door of the safe open. He told her, "I don't open this often. Jeff takes care of it most of the time." He reached inside and brought out an attaché-type case with a leather covering and handle. Placing it on the desk, he opened it. "This is the Book of Gospels," he told her.

Clare studied the fabulous manuscript and saw the ornate gold, green and red lettering of its first page. "It was all done by hand!" she marveled.

"Yes. Copied before the days of printing," he said. "The monks did the script, and the Nun of Valencia supplied the drawings." He turned the pages of the manuscript, and she had a chance to see the numerous colorful yet fairly tiny illustrations of many New Testament scenes.

She felt a strange sense of uneasiness as she studied the ancient manuscript. The knowledge that possession of it had brought about so many deaths was upsetting. She said, "Is it true she lost her eyesight as a result of the long years of work on this manuscript?"

"That is the legend," Uncle Benjamin said with a slight frown. "And that legend is linked with the curse. Your Aunt Winifred nags me continually to give this to Bedford University. But my friend, Professor Curtis, is very reluctant to accept it. He fears the dark history of the Book of Gospels."

She said, "I met Professor Curtis yesterday."

"So I heard," her uncle said. "What do you think of him?"

"He has a sense of humor. He seems very wise."

"He is," Uncle Benjamin said. "I'm to meet him at the university this morning. He first wanted it to be at ten, but I've arranged to arrive there about eleven. I preferred to wait until Jeff returned; then if any phone calls of importance come in, he'll be here to answer them."

Clare was still thinking about the stark tragedy associated with the Book of Gospels. She watched him shut the attaché case and return it to the safe. She asked, "Have you made up your mind what you're going to do with that manuscript?"

"Not yet," he said. "I wish I could. I feel my life is in constant danger as long as I own it."

Clare said, "And doesn't that also mean danger for those around you?"

"Surely," he agreed. "That young Frenchman who acted as my associate for a while died trying to save the manuscript."

"I should have thought you'd have wanted to get rid of it then," she suggested.

He was on his knees before the safe again. "You don't realize what an important possession it is. While I own the Book of Gospels, I'm assured of being included in any newspaper or magazine articles dealing with the world of valuable books."

"And that is so important to you?"

"As a collector, yes," he said. He reached in the safe again and brought out a small volume bound in light calfskin. "This one has a long title: 'Narrative of the Most Extraordinary and Distressing Shipwreck of the Whale Ship Essex of Nantucket; Which was Attacked and Finally Destroyed by a Large Spermacetti Whale, in the Pacific Ocean.' Its author was Owen Chase, a member of the ship's crew on the hazardous voyage. It was owned once by Herman Melville, the author of 'Moby Dick,' and contains pages of written notes in his hand. It's doubtful if he'd ever have written his novel if he hadn't come upon this volume."

She was impressed by the story. "Every one of

the books seem to have some strange history," she said.

"There's a story linked with most of them," he agreed. "I have other precious items in here, but I won't take the time to show them to you just now."

"I've enjoyed what I've seen," she said.

Uncle Benjamin closed the safe and locked it. "On my death, these volumes will either be given to the university or auctioned. In either case, they will be an important part of my estate."

He went back to the task of bringing down the Kipling volumes and dusting them. The way he lovingly went over each book revealed how much they meant to him. Clare helped him with the task, wondering where Winifred Rand was. This went on for a half-hour, and then Jeff returned.

While the young librarian and her uncle were discussing the business Jeff had transacted at the bank, she took the opportunity of going upstairs to her room. As she reached her door, she saw that it was slightly ajar, and she halted. The door had been left closed, and seeing it this way gave her an odd sensation.

After a moment, she took the knob in her hand and opened the door. Standing by the window was Winifred Rand. The big, dark-haired woman looked somewhat guilty as Clare went into the room.

"Oh, there you are!" Winifred said.

"Yes," Clare said quietly.

"I was looking for you. And I decided to come up here," the older woman told her.

Clare said, "I was in the library with Uncle Benjamin."

"Were you?" The older woman pretended innocence. "Wasn't that stupid of me! It was the one place I didn't look."

"I've been there all morning."

"Benjamin is so single-minded," Winifred Rand said. "You mustn't let him work you too hard."

"I enjoy the books."

"I'm glad," her aunt said. "Benjamin needs someone who really shares his interest in collecting. I must confess I don't. Not that I try to discourage him. But I'm no help. As his niece, you're like a child to him, a child of his own! It's very nice."

"I hope I can be of some value to him," she said. "Otherwise I might as well have not come here."

"That is so," the dark-haired woman said with an unexpected show of consideration. The eyes behind her horn-rimmed glasses were almost frightened. Winifred was giving every evidence of guilt. She went on to say, "I came to ask you about last night."

"What about it?" Clare asked.

"Did you tell my husband what happened?"

"No. I decided not to for the moment. It seems he's worried enough as it is."

"I agree," Winifred Rand said. "He's not himself. His health has been poor lately. There's no reason to worry him about last night's little escapade."

"I felt it was more than that."

Winifred was clearly becoming more nervous. "It was indeed a nasty business but it could have been the result of a nightmare on your part."

"I don't think so."

"I'd like to believe it was."

"Yet that doesn't make it so," Clare said dryly. "I'm sure somebody lured me into the hall with the sole purpose of attacking me."

"But why?"

"To get me out of the way. Someone doesn't want me here."

The dark woman with the glasses became flustered again. "I'm positive you're wrong about that. Your uncle and I were both delighted to have you come live with us."

"Perhaps someone else is not so happy about it."

"But who?" Winifred Rand wanted to know. "There are not that many others in the house. You can't suspect Jeff or Mrs. Fox. You just don't have that many to consider."

Clare asked, "What about the ghost?"

The eyes behind the glasses met hers uneasily. "You mean the avenging nun?"

"Yes."

"It could be," the older woman admitted lamely. "I always try to close my mind to the ghost."

"But you have seen her?" Clare persisted.

The older woman had gone pale. "Yes," she said in a small voice. "I have seen her."

"Did she threaten you?"

"She gave me a bad scare," Winifred admitted. "I was on this floor. It was late at night. I'd come up to try and find Jeff. Later, I learned he'd gone out. I was about to start back down the stairs when this shadowy gray figure appeared before me on the landing. I almost fainted."

"And then what?"

"It evaporated before my eyes; just vanished into thin air. And it had been solid enough for me to distinguish the flowing gray habit and the hood over her face. Then in the next few seconds she had gone."

"But she didn't touch you?"

"No. But in the stories connected with the Book

of Gospels, they claim the ghost actually killed people."

"That's what I understood," Clare said.

Winifred nodded. "So she could very well have shoved you down the stairs last night."

"So it seems," Clare said.

"You're feeling all right this morning?"

"Yes, except for a few bruises."

"That's what I wanted to find out," the older woman said. "As long as you weren't seriously hurt, I think it might be best to say nothing about what happened."

"I'm not sure." Clare decided not to tell her she'd already discussed her accident with Jeff, and that he'd informed her he'd seen Mrs. Fox in the lower rear hallway.

Winifred moved toward the door. "I think it would be a wise decision to keep silent," she said. "If it was the ghost, it would only distress my husband."

"I suppose so," Clare said, pretending to go along with the suggestion. "What about Mrs. Fox?"

The older woman looked frightened again. "I asked Mrs. Fox if she'd heard any unusual sounds last night, and she said no. She'd slept soundly."

Clare knew that either Winifred or the housekeeper had to be lying, and she had an idea it was Winifred. She had Jeff's definite statement that he'd seen Mrs. Fox at about the time of the midnight episode.

She said, "I still find it strange that she didn't hear me scream."

"Her room is a long distance away from the front stairs," Winifred pointed out.

"Yes," Clare said in a dubious tone. "You mentioned that last night."

"So I did," Winifred said uneasily. "Well, I must get along. I only wanted to make sure you were suffering no serious effects from the fall. Think over what I've suggested."

"I will," Clare said as the older woman went out, leaving her alone. She stood there for a moment in a troubled mood. She was almost certain that either Winifred or Mrs. Fox had been guilty of the attempt on her life. And she thought that Winifred's story about seeing the ghost had been a phony one, made up for her benefit, so she would think she'd been the victim of an attack by the fabled Nun of Valencia.

CHAPTER FIVE

Clare returned to the library in the afternoon and worked with Jeff. He was again doing repairs on some of the Byron volumes, while she continued to dust the Rudyard Kipling collection and replace them on the shelves. Her uncle had gone out to meet Professor Curtis and was not expected back until dinner time.

She didn't want to discuss her conversation with Winifred in the library, as there was too great a chance of them being overheard. But she hoped that later she and Jeff might go out somewhere and she could speak to him frankly.

It seemed the young man must have read her mind, because he interrupted his work to say, "Would you enjoy going to the Prudential Tower tonight? They have jazz music and a nice lounge."

"I'd enjoy it," she said. "It should offer a lovely view of Boston."

"Possibly the best available," he agreed. "There'll be no special hurry. We don't have to leave until nine."

"Fine," she said. "Some day soon I want to do the rounds of the historical spots in this area. I'd also like to visit some stores."

"You can go any time," Jeff said with a smile. "Your position here is a purely honorary one. Your uncle wants you here for your company rather than for the work you can do in connection with the library."

"I still want to do my share," she said. She'd finished with the last of the Kipling volumes and was on her way across the room when she paused to glance out the window. Standing directly across the street was a shabbily dressed, gray-haired man with dark glasses. He was staring up at the library windows in a rather strange way.

Jeff noticed the change in her expression as she spotted the stranger, and he asked, "Something interesting out there?"

She gave him a quick, troubled glance. "Yes. There's a man on the opposite sidewalk. He seems to be staring up at these windows."

Jeff smiled. "Why not? He's seen you in the window and is admiring a pretty girl."

"He was doing it before I came to the window," she said worriedly. "Take a look at him."

Jeff came over beside her and gazed out at the man in the dark blue topcoat and crumpled soft gray hat. "I have an idea I've seen him somewhere before," he said.

"He's not a type one is liable to forget," Clare said, still staring at the man, whose long gray hair spilled unevenly over his coat collar and who wore large black-lensed glasses which gave him an odd blank appearance.

"And he is taking a lot of interest in this house," Jeff agreed.

"I wonder why."

"Hard to tell," Jeff said. "Maybe for no good reason. There are a lot of eccentrics who drift up from the Charles Street section."

"He's moving along now," she said, watching the shabbily dressed man walking slowly up the hill.

"Must watch for him again," Jeff said.

"Yes." She went over to the tall ladder and mounted it to place the books back on the upper shelf. When she came down again she asked him, "Where do you have dinner? You don't dine with my uncle and aunt at Pierre's."

Jeff paused in his work. "I go to a modest little restaurant on Charles Street. They serve plain food, which I like, and the prices are less than at Pierre's."

"Sounds as if you'd found yourself a good alternative," she said.

They worked in the library until five-thirty, and then she left to go up to her room and change. When she was on the way out, a stern-faced Mrs. Fox came to meet her in the hallway. She had several letters in her hand.

"These came for you in the afternoon mail," she said in her cold fashion.

"Thank you," Clare said, and took the letters. They were from girl friends in Chicago who'd promised to write her.

"I meant to get them to you sooner," Mrs. Fox said, "but things kept interfering."

"I wouldn't have had time to read them until now in any case," Clare said. And she went upstairs with the letters.

When she returned downstairs, she found both Winifred and her uncle waiting for her to go to Pierre's with them. They left the house and walked the few steps to the restaurant.

"This is very convenient," Clare said as they entered.

Winifred nodded. "Yes, and the food is excellent."

Pierre Reaux was on hand, a smiling host, to take them to a white-clothed table in the rear of the big room which had been made by tearing out all the walls on that floor. When they were seated and had given their orders, they began to talk.

Uncle Benjamin complained, "I give up my day to help Professor Curtis at the university, and he leaves me early in the afternoon."

Winifred asked, "Had it been arranged for you to be there the entire day?"

"Until four in the afternoon," the gray-haired Benjamin said. "Then he discovered he had a prior appointment and rushed off at two-thirty. I spent the balance of the time with his assistant, but it wasn't the same. I wasn't able to accomplish so much."

"Are you an advisor for the university collection?" Clare asked.

"Yes," her uncle said. "Ever since I retired some years ago, I've given my time to them."

Winifred tossed her head indignantly. "For which you get precious little thanks."

"I don't do it for thanks," Benjamin said. "I enjoy it."

"I should think you'd devote a little more time to me and our home," his wife complained.

Benjamin Rand gave her a stony glance. "I don't believe I've ever neglected you," he said. And then, almost ignoring her, he turned to Clare and commented, "I believe you share some of my enthusiasm about books."

She smiled. "I'm beginning to find them fascinating. Of course I'm a novice when it comes to collecting."

"Utterly fascinating," her uncle said with enthusiasm. "At the university this afternoon, I actually held in my hands an autographed copy of Edgar Allan Poe's 'Murders in the Rue Morgue' in pamphlet form."

Winifred smiled coldly. "It pains me to think of the thousands of dollars the university must have spent for it. I think the money could be put to much better use."

"I disagree," her husband said. "You simply don't appreciate the value of these items in the records of our culture."

"I'm afraid I don't," his wife said.

Their dinners were served, and Clare was relieved that the conversation turned to food. She was well along with dinner when she glanced down the room and was startled. Sitting facing them, at a small table near the wall, was the same elderly man with dark glasses whom she'd seen earlier staring up at the library windows.

She touched her uncle on the arm and said, "That man with the dark glasses sitting alone—do you know him?"

Benjamin Rand paused to look in the direction she'd indicated. After a moment, he said, "Strange! His face is familiar, and yet I don't believe I've ever seen him before. Why did you ask?"

"This afternoon he stood on the sidewalk opposite the house and stared up at the library windows, for an unusually long while."

"I wonder why," Benjamin said with a frown.

Winifred had also glanced at the man. "He seems a harmless enough type," she said. "Perhaps his standing there was only a coincidence. You just thought he was staring at the windows. He could have been resting on his way up the hill."

"Perhaps," Clare said. "But I don't think so."

Benjamin Rand said, "It may be someone who has read about my collection and the house. A lot of articles have appeared in the press."

"I call them invitations to thievery," Winifred said in her arrogant fashion. She seemed to have regained all her old poise. The nervousness she'd exhibited earlier in the day, when talking to Clare, had vanished.

Clare's uncle said, "Perhaps Pierre may know who the fellow is. I'll ask him on our way out."

"That might be a good idea," Clare agreed. "If he's a regular customer, Pierre is almost certain to remember his name."

They finished dinner, and on the way out her uncle halted to chat with Pierre a moment, while Clare and Winifred walked on. They had reached the entrance foyer of the Mount Vernon Street house before Benjamin Rand caught up with them.

He said, "I asked Pierre. And what do you think?"

"I can't imagine," Winifred said. "Do go on."

"This fellow is a retired lawyer, and he's rented Pierre's basement apartment. Been there for several months, from what Pierre told me. Apparently he's a quiet man and minds his own business. He's a bachelor and takes most of his meals at the restaurant, just as we do."

Winifred said, "At least that explains who he is and what he's doing in the neighborhood. I dislike making a mystery of everything."

Clare knew this was directed at her.

However, she merely said, "At least we know where he lives."

Her uncle nodded. "I must try and find out his name and more about him."

They sat in the drawing room conversing for a while, and then Jeff arrived to take her out on the date they'd arranged earlier. As she left with the slender young man, she thought she caught a look of displeasure on Winifred's face. It further underlined her belief that at least one of her enemies in the old mansion was her uncle's wife.

They walked down the hill to Charles Street, and Jeff held up his hand to flag a taxi. It was several minutes before one stopped for them. He gave the driver the address where they wanted to go, and they sat back in the taxi to relax.

She turned to him in the semi-darkness of the taxi and asked, "Did you notice the look on Winifred's face when we left?"

He considered. "Come to think of it, she didn't seemed too pleased."

"She fairly glowered at us," Clare said. "Do you think she has an idea we're conspiring against her?"

Jeff said, "She sometimes gets strange ideas."

"I'm all too aware of that," Clare said. And she went on to tell him about seeing the man with the dark glasses at Pierre's. She finished by giving Winifred's reaction to the incident. "She made a point of suggesting I'd tried to create a mystery out of the incident."

"You were right," Jeff said. "That man acted strangely. How could she judge when she didn't see him?"

"I don't think she was worried about being fair. It was a chance to strike at me."

"I'm worried about that fellow," Jeff said, "and more so now that I know he's a neighbor. And you say he's in the basement under the café?"

"Yes."

"He'll bear watching. I can't see him as a retired lawyer."

She gave the young man a worried glance. "Do you think he might be some kind of maniac?"

"Stranger things have been known. Remember the Boston strangler?"

She gave a shudder. "I read accounts about those murders. That was enough."

"In a city as large as this, strange types gather. You want to be careful when you go out of the house alone. That fellow may be watching you, waiting for a chance to get you by yourself."

"You think I'm the reason for his interest and not the house?"

"I'm afraid that's what I'll have to believe until I find out some other reason for his actions," Jeff said.

"Now I'm really upset," Clare told him.

"It's just a matter of being cautious until we're sure about him," was Jeff's opinion.

They had been paying little attention to the cab as it wended its way through the busy streets of the city. Now they were at the modern Prudential Center. The cab halted before an enormous flight of steps leading up to the plaza, and Jeff paid his fare and tip. They left the cab and walked up the granite steps to the main area of the plaza with its many buildings. For a few minutes they window-shopped in the various stores and then Jeff led Clare to an express elevator which swiftly took them up the fifty-odd stories to the top of the center.

They emerged in the lounge area, which was crowded and where the orchestra was already playing. The waiter found them a table beside one of the many windows overlooking the city far below. When they had ordered, Jeff smiled at her.

"What do you have to match this in Chicago?" he wanted to know.

"We have a few skyscraper restaurants," she

said, defending the windy city. "And I lived a much less tense existence when I was there."

Jeff's handsome face showed his admiration for her. "Give us a little time, and we'll make your Boston surroundings more pleasant."

"I don't know." She frowned. "Things seem to be getting worse. It's plain Winifred considers me an intruder and a nuisance. Last night I was attacked, and today a possible maniac fastens his attention on me. What next?"

"Did you tell your uncle about last night?"

"No. I thought I might at dinner. But then Winifred came along," she said despairingly.

"I've been going over it in my mind," the young man said. "I think you should tell him. Benjamin should know all that is happening in the house. Too often he doesn't."

"I'll discuss it with him in the morning," she promised.

The waitress came with their drinks, and they listened to the music and noted the groups at the adjoining tables. They were mostly young people like themselves, out for an evening of enjoyment.

Jeff asked, "Have you any other ideas about last night?"

"I don't know. Winifred came to my room today and questioned me about how I felt. She seemed very nervous."

"That's interesting."

"I thought so. And she was insistent that I should not bother Uncle Benjamin about the incident."

"That could also mean something," Jeff said.

"My own impression," she agreed. "And when I asked her about Mrs. Fox, she claimed the housekeeper had slept through it all."

Jeff frowned. "I know that isn't so!"

"Exactly."

"I wonder what it adds up to," he said with a sigh.

"Could Mrs. Fox have played the phantom and attacked me on Winifred's instructions?" she said.

He smiled wryly. "It's pretty dramatic, but I suppose it is barely possible."

"Anything is possible, it seems."

"Winifred is playing some kind of game," Jeff said. "It will take time to find out what it is."

"And meanwhile, I'm the target for her underhanded action," she said with some bitterness.

"It may be," he admitted. "I'm not sure."

"We discussed the possibility of my being the victim of a ghostly attack."

"How did she seem to feel about that?"

Clare grimaced. "She gave me the impression that she felt it might have been the legendary nun who attacked me. And then she told me a long story about having seen it. I had the feeling the story was made up for my benefit."

"It may have been," Jeff said.

"She made it very graphic. But I was left with doubts. Still, there was that business of my jewelry being moved about in my room."

"I know," he said, looking serious. "And there have been other happenings of the same nature in the house. Lately I've come upon books which have been moved around and changed to different places."

"Could Uncle Benjamin have moved them?"

"No. And he and I are the only ones who place the books. It's a mystery, like your jewelry being moved. There just isn't any logical explanation for it. So you have to blame the ghost."

Her eyes met his solemnly. "You think she moved the books?"

"Who else?"

"That's what you'll have to find out," she said, "just as I have to try and discover a few things. If we fail, we can always fall back on the Nun of Valencia as our final solution to the mysteries of the old house."

Jeff smiled wryly. "At least you're approaching the problem with a minimum of superstition. I'll be interested in your conclusions."

Clare gave a resigned sigh. "At the moment I just want to survive so I may come to a few."

They remained at the lounge for almost two hours and then took a cab back to the house in Mount Vernon Street. As always at the midnight hour, the house was silent and dimly lighted. They walked up the front steps, and Jeff unlocked the door that let them enter the lower foyer.

"It was a good evening," he told her with a smile.

"I always enjoy myself with you," she told him.

"I feel the same way," he said. "In fact, as soon as we leave this house, I find myself in an entirely different mood."

"I know," she said, smiling up at him.

He looked at her earnestly. "Do you mind if I'm very frank?"

"I don't think so."

"All right," he said. "Although we've known each other for such a short time, I believe I'm in love with you."

She said, "That's sweet of you, Jeff."

He studied her in bewilderment. "That's no comment. Tell me how you feel about me."

Clare's tone was gentle. "It's possible I feel exactly the same way."

Jeff looked delighted and took her in his arms for a long kiss. When he let her go, he said, "I had to tell you. I'm afraid you might decide to leave suddenly and would never know."

"I'm all the more anxious to stay here now," she said. "But until we've cleared up some of the secrets of this house, we really can't settle for romance."

He shook his head. "You're so practical! Try being a romantic for a change!"

"I will as soon as I solve the mysteries here."

Jeff looked bleak. "Some of them have gone on for centuries."

"They still can be solved."

"I wish you luck," Jeff said unhappily. "But I have the idea our romance is going to be deferred for an awfully long while!"

He saw her upstairs to her room and then went on down the hall in the direction of his own bedroom.

She quickly got ready for bed and then turned out the lights. She was tired, and she was almost asleep when she heard a familiar sound.

There was a gentle knocking on her door, and then her name was whispered as it had been before. "Clare!"

She sat up, fully awake and trembling slightly. She called out, "Who's there?"

There was no reply. This time the knock and the whisper had come only once. She waited and began to wonder if she hadn't imagined it. But she knew that she hadn't. The phantom caller had stopped at her door once again.

Her curiosity began to outweigh her judgment, and she got out of bed and made her way to the door. She listened for a moment, then opened the door and went outside into the near-darkness of the corridor.

CHAPTER SIX

Clare was clad only in her nightgown, and her feet were bare. She'd hurried out of bed without even putting on her slippers. She trembled slightly as she stood in the shadows of the hall, expecting at any moment to see some phantom figure. But thus far she seemed to be alone.

She was about to turn and go back into her bedroom, putting the entire incident down to nerves, when from the end of the corridor the whisper came again, very clear this time!

"Clare!"

Like a person in a trance, she began moving forward in the darkness, her eyes wide with fear. She walked slowly until she reached the stairway. Then, grasping the stair rail, she began descending the stairs to the third floor level, where her uncle and aunt had their bedrooms. Everything was silent and dark on the third floor.

But now, as she stood on the brink of the stairway which would take her to the library on the second floor, she saw a glow of light from the library. Someone must be down there in the middle of the night. But who? Hardly the avenging nun! Phantoms didn't need light!

Very deliberately she began walking down the stairs. She paused at almost every step, and once, when she thought she heard a sound from behind her, she turned around quickly, her heart pounding. But there was no one there; just the shadows and that deathly quiet.

So she continued on down to the second floor. Light was streaming from the door of the library. Taut with fear, she crossed to the doorway to see who might be there. And then she came to a sudden halt. Panic welled up in her, but she was unable either to scream or to move. Stretched out on the library floor, at the bottom of the tall ladder used to reach the top bookshelves, was the motionless figure of her Uncle Benjamin. The gray-haired man had on his dressing gown over his pajamas. A book had escaped his hand, which was still reaching out for it on the hardwood floor.

It was a shocking tableau and one that stunned her for several seconds. Then she came out of shock and began to scream. She kept on screaming until Jeff came to join her, followed by Winifred and, lastly, Mrs. Fox. The housekeeper tried to placate her and halt the sobbing which had followed the screams as Jeff went over to examine her uncle.

Jeff returned in a moment, his handsome face white with shock. He said, "He's alive, but I'll have to get a doctor and have him taken to a hospital at once. He seems to have had a shock!"

"Get Dr. Greensmith," Winifred told him. "I don't want my husband sent to a hospital unless it's absolutely required. He hates hospitals!"

"I can't argue that now," Jeff said. "I'll get Dr. Greensmith on the phone." He hurried over to the desk and lifted up the phone.

Winifred came to Clare. "How did you know

about this? What were you doing down here?" Her tone was accusing.

Clare was becoming calmer. She said, "I heard a knock on my door, like last night, and my name was called. I followed the voice down here and found him."

Winifred glared at her. "Do you expect me to believe that?"

"It's true!" the girl declared.

Winifred's reaction was to give her an angry look, cross to her husband's prone body and kneel by it. Mrs. Fox, in nightgown and robe, looked shaken.

She turned to Clare and asked, "Was he on the floor, as he is now, when you came in here first?"

"Yes."

"So you didn't talk to him at all?" the housekeeper asked.

"No." Clare was only half-listening, her other self taking in Jeff's frantic conversation on the phone. He was having a hard time convincing Dr. Greensmith that he should come to the house on Mount Vernon Street at once.

Mrs. Fox said, "Then you don't know whether he was attacked or had a spell and toppled off the ladder?"

"I'm afraid not," she admitted.

Jeff went over to kneel by her uncle again. Then, after a minute or two, he left Winifred to remain with her husband while he rose and came to Clare.

There was a tortured look in his eyes. "I couldn't feel worse about this if it had happened to my father. Actually, Benjamin Rand was a father figure to me."

"I know," she said. "Is the doctor coming?"

"After I almost had to threaten him. I don't know how long it will be before he arrives."

Mrs. Fox spoke up. "Dr. Greensmith doesn't live far from here. He ought to be here within a quarter of an hour. He can walk from his place to here."

Jeff said, "I hope you're right. Benjamin could die while he's waiting for medical aid."

"You've done the best thing," Clare encouraged him.

"I'd like to think so, but if we lose Benjamin I'll never forgive myself."

"You can't blame yourself, no matter what happens," Clare told him.

Mrs. Fox drew her robe about her. "I'll go down to the front door and turn on the lights. As soon as Dr. Greensmith arrives, I'll let him in and bring him up here."

"Good idea," Jeff told the housekeeper, and Mrs. Fox hurried off.

From her kneeling position by her prostrate husband, Winifred wailed, "I think he's stopped breathing!"

Jeff quickly returned to the side of the injured man. He leaned his head against his chest and listened. After a while he rose, telling Winifred, "You were wrong that time. He's still alive and breathing, even though the breathing is faint."

Winifred was getting more frantic every moment. "Why doesn't that doctor come?"

"Give him time!" Jeff said sharply as he returned to Clare.

Clare said, "What seems to be wrong with him?"

"Difficult to tell. I think it's a stroke."

She looked at her uncle on the floor, with Winifred bending over him. It seemed like some dreadful nightmare.

She said, "Mightn't he have fallen from the ladder?"

Jeff nodded. "Or he might have been maliciously toppled from the ladder," he pointed out.

Her eyes widened. "Do you think that may be what happened?"

"I can't tell," he said. "We need the doctor."

"Uncle Benjamin couldn't have been warned of danger," she said. "He didn't cry out!"

"No," Jeff said. "If he had, one of us would surely have heard him."

"I wouldn't have come and found him if it hadn't been for that ghostly whisper," she said. "It summoned me to the hall again."

"And you obeyed it? You realize what a terrible chance you took?"

"I know. I seemed to forget about the danger; all I could think of was the voice."

"So you came down here in search of it?"

She nodded. "Yes. I seemed to be hypnotized!"

"You're lucky to be alive," he said grimly.

"There wasn't a sound in here when I entered the room, and then I saw my uncle on the floor!" She halted, and her eyes filled with tears again.

"Pull yourself together," Jeff urged her. "Having hysterics isn't going to help."

"I can't help it," she said. "This has been an awful experience."

Jeff glanced back at the still unconscious book collector. "I never thought I'd see him like this."

"How long has he been unconscious?" she worried.

The young man's face was grim. "I don't think Winifred will be able to help us. Perhaps the doctor can give us some idea when the stroke seized him."

"If it was a stroke!"

There was a ring of the front doorbell, and Mrs. Fox's excited tones mixed with a deep masculine voice. The voices drew nearer as the doctor mounted the stairs. Then he came through the library doorway, a big bald man with a broad face which was now concerned.

"What's been happening here?" he demanded.

Winifred was on her feet and came running to him. "Dr. Greensmith! My husband!"

He gave her a sharp glance. "You must be brave," he said, and went over to the man on the floor, kneeling beside him and opening his doctor's bag. The examination took several minutes. Then Dr. Greensmith rose and turned to them.

"Mr. Rand has had a stroke," he said. "It is too early for me to say whether it was a mild one or a more serious attack. The best thing is to get him to a hospital."

"No!" Winifred protested. "I don't want him in a hospital."

The doctor frowned at her. "Your husband is very ill and still unconscious."

"We can afford around-the-clock nurses and every care," Winifred argued. "Benjamin has a fear of and an aversion to hospitals. He'll never forgive me if I allow him to be taken to one. He can be cared for here, can't he?"

Dr. Greensmith looked concerned and a little angry. "It will be risky and a great deal of trouble for everyone. I don't recommend it!"

"I will not let him be taken from the house!" Winifred declared.

Clare moved forward toward her. "Perhaps you should listen to the doctor," she warned the older woman.

Winifred's face was crimson with anger. "No!"

Dr. Greensmith asked Clare, "Who are you?"

"I'm his niece."

"And I'm his secretary," Jeff said, joining her.

"I can't recall Mr. Rand ever having said he didn't want to be a hospital patient."

Winifred turned on him indignantly. "Are you saying that you know more about my husband's wishes than I do?"

"No," Jeff said, taken back by her rage. "I'm simply telling the truth as I know it."

"It's something you don't know anything about!" she challenged him.

Dr. Greensmith raised a hand to silence him. "We have a dangerously ill man here. I can't stand by while you argue among yourselves. I will reluctantly accept the instructions of the patient's wife. But there is no time to lose. He must be put in a bed at once and given certain medications and care. Once he is in bed, I'll contact my nursing agency and see if a nurse is available."

His declaration brought them all to a realization that Benjamin Rand might not live. Dr. Greensmith, Jeff, Clare and Mrs. Fox carried the dead weight of the unconscious man upstairs. There Winifred saw him placed in bed and sat at his bedside while Dr. Greensmith went out of the room to phone the nursing agency.

Jeff and Clare left the shadowy room with its single light on a dresser and Winifred seated, grieving, at the bedside of her husband. They were both still in something of a state of shock.

In the hallway, Jeff turned to Clare and said in a low voice, "I wonder what that performance meant."

"I have no idea," she said.

Jeff was frowning. "I know Benjamin wasn't afraid of hospitals."

"Then why did she insist he was?"

"For her own reasons, whatever they may be," Jeff said grimly. "I'm beginning to wonder if she didn't follow him into the library and cause his fall and subsequent stroke."

"We'll not know that unless he comes around."

Jeff gave her a meaningful look. "And that is probably the last thing she wants him to do. She may fear sending him to a hospital because she thinks he could recover there."

"It's a dreadful accusation," she reminded him. "She seemed genuinely broken up by Uncle Benjamin's condition."

"All that could be a smooth acting job," he warned her.

Clare was shocked by his cold reasoning.

The doctor came down the corridor and joined them. His broad face was perplexed. "I can't think what has gotten into Mrs. Rand's head. She is making this very difficult for all of us and definitely cutting down her husband's chances of recovery."

Clare said, "Can't you send my uncle to a hospital, in spite of her arguments?"

"I could," Dr. Greensmith said. "But it's a tricky case. If he should die, she'd blame me. And the chances are against his recovering, whether home or at the hospital. In these desperate circumstances, I'll not cross her."

Jeff asked, "Did you get a nurse?"

"I'll have one here in an hour," the doctor said. "In the meantime, I'll medicate the patient and watch him myself. I'll have nurses around the clock. It's the only solution."

Clare said, "Have you any idea what brought on the stroke?"

He shook his head. "It could have been coming on for weeks. Or it may have been brought on suddenly by a sudden shock and the fall from the ladder. He has a bad bruise on one side of his face and at the temple."

Jeff asked, "Is there anything we can do?"

The doctor nodded. "Get me some coffee. I was dragged out of bed, and I'm not sure I'm completely awake yet."

He went on into the room where Winifred sat with her husband. Jeff turned to Clare and said, "We'll go to the kitchen."

When they got there, they found the housekeeper had already put on a pot of coffee and the hot drink was ready. She left with a tray for the doctor, and Jeff and Clare sat down to hot coffee in the kitchen.

Jeff stirred the sugar in his steaming cup and said, "I still don't get it. You heard what the doctor said. The stroke may have been brought on by a sudden shock and the fall from the ladder."

"Yes," she said, sipping her coffee, which was black and bitter.

"Wouldn't that fit in with Winifred going to the library after him and causing his fall?"

"I suppose so," she said solemnly. "It would also fit in with something else."

"What?"

"The ghost legend."

Jeff stared at her. "You think the ghost got to him?"

"She has, to the other owners of the Book of Gospels."

He nodded grimly. "You're right."

"There have been other signs of her visitations in this old house," she said.

Jeff looked shaken. "So the Nun of Valencia eventually got her revenge!"

"Only my uncle can tell us that."

"If we said anything to the doctor about the

ghost, he'd say we were crazy," Jeff said dismally.

"We can take that for granted. Still, we mustn't eliminate the possibility my uncle is a victim of the curse."

"You're right," Jeff agreed. "I've been talking about it all along, and so has your uncle and Winifred."

She gave Jeff a knowing look. "You told me the chief reason he had me come here from Chicago was his belief that the ghost would soon cause his death."

"He told me that one day," Jeff said. "I said it was nonsense. But I suppose in a way I was touched by the superstition just as much as he was." He paused. "Have you ever seen the manuscript?"

"He showed it to me."

"Then maybe you'll understand what I mean when I say it always gave me a spooky feeling to handle it and look at it," Jeff said earnestly.

She recalled her own uneasy feeling at the sight of the manuscript and sighed. "Yes. I know."

Jeff got up and began to pace back and forth on the tile floor of the kitchen. "There has to be something in the legend. I believe the ghost of that nun has made its presence felt here. Winifred knows it, too, and so she may be using the knowledge to confuse us and cover up a crime for which she is responsible."

"That is something we'll have to decide."

He gave her a bitter look. "The mystery grows deeper!"

Mrs. Fox returned to the kitchen. The sight of her stern, pale face made it plain that this was not the time or place to continue their conversation. They went back upstairs, leaving the housekeeper to her own domain. Dr. Greensmith was still in the patient's room, and so was Winifred.

They sat in silence on a love seat on the landing. Little was said; they were both in a troubled, thoughtful mood. The nurse arrived, and Jeff let her in and took her to the sickroom.

About a half-hour later, Dr. Greensmith came downstairs. He turned to Jeff and Clare, who had descended into the lower foyer to speak with him before he left.

He told them, "There has been no change in the patient's condition."

Jeff said, "How long before we can expect one?"

Dr. Greensmith considered. "Perhaps by tomorrow. He can get better or worse. It's my guess he's had a fairly massive shock. If he recovers, there will be definite impairment for at least a period, perhaps permanently."

Clare said, "If he lives through the next few days, would you consider it a good sign?"

"I would find it most encouraging," the doctor agreed. "I have made arrangements for the nurses, and I will call here on my way to the hospital in the early morning. I still think it is wrong to keep him here. But there's little we can do unless Mrs. Rand changes her mind."

"Thank you, Doctor," Clare said as she saw him out.

When she came back into the foyer, Jeff was standing there, looking grim. "I'm afraid your uncle isn't going to live," he said. "The doctor didn't seem hopeful."

"He gave us the facts," she said. "There's always the chance Uncle Benjamin will come around. He seemed in good health before this happened."

"That makes it even stranger," Jeff said darkly.

"Perhaps we can persuade Winifred to allow him to be moved to a hospital tomorrow," she suggested.

Jeff frowned. "I wouldn't count on it."

"We can try."

The young man seemed to have a sudden thought. "We've missed one good bet. I should have phoned Dr. Curtis at once. He is your uncle's best friend, and he has a certain amount of influence with Winifred."

"You mean Professor Curtis of the university?"

"Yes."

"Can you reach him at this time of night?"

He nodded. "I have his private number. If he is at home, we ought to be able to wake him up."

"Should we?"

"I think so, yes," Jeff decided. "He'd want to know about this. If I hadn't been so shaken, I'd have thought of it before. He could be our best hope."

"Then call him," she agreed.

"I have his phone listed in the library," Jeff said. "We'll have to go up there."

They hurried up the stairs and into the library. She tried to avoid looking at the spot where they'd found the unconscious body of her uncle. Jeff was already at his desk, checking his private telephone listing. He found the number and at once dialed it. There was a long, sickening wait as the phone rang at the other end of the line, and they kept hoping the professor would answer it.

At last Jeff put down the phone with a despairing gesture. "No use," he said. "Either we can't wake him, or he's out of the city on a lecture trip. He quite often gives lectures at other universities."

"The idea is still good," she said by way of encouragement. "He'll surely be back in the morning, and you can get him at the university then."

"We'll hope so," Jeff said grimly. "If our luck is really out, he'll be away on a trip."

"Don't think about it."

"I won't," he said. "I'll call again early tomorrow. I'm sure he can help us."

"He'd be another voice of reason," she said.

At that moment she was aware that someone else had entered the library. She turned and saw that it was Winifred. The dark-haired woman was deathly pale and looked like a ghost in her white dressing gown. Her eyes behind the horn-rimmed glasses held a malevolent gleam.

"What are you two conspiring to use against me now?" she demanded.

Jeff took a step toward her. "You're wrong if you think we are your enemies. We only want to help."

"That is true," Clare said.

Winifred smiled scornfully at them. "Do you think I believe that? You tried to turn the doctor against me tonight, knowing that my husband is dying!"

"We want to save Uncle Benjamin, and we think the hospital is the best place for him!" Clare exclaimed.

"What either of you think is of little concern to me," the older woman said scornfully.

"You make that clear," Jeff said in a bitter tone.

"I'll make it even more so," Winifred said in acid tones. "You two will either accept my edicts in this house from now on or get out of here!"

CHAPTER SEVEN

Clare and Jeff said very little as they went back up to the fourth floor and their rooms. As they parted, he gave her a brief kiss and reminded her that they planned to get in touch with Professor Alan Curtis as early as possible in the morning. He now seemed their best hope in bringing reason back to the house.

Clare slept fitfully for the rest of the night and awoke early. She did not go downstairs at once but spent some time in her room. Staring out of the window, she could see some of the early morning business people striding along the distant sidewalk of Charles Street. She found herself wondering if this was to be the end of her Boston adventure. If her Uncle Benjamin died, there would be no reason for her to remain in the house on Mount Vernon Street.

And unless he had already named her in his will, she was sure she'd get short shrift from the arrogant Winifred. The day was bleak and gray, in tune with her mood. She was sure Jeff would also be dismissed in the event of her uncle's death. Most of the book collection would go to Bedford

University, and Winifred would soon get rid of the rest.

She also worried about her uncle's condition but assumed there had been no change in it, since she'd heard no word. At last she went downstairs to breakfast. And seated at the table was a wan-looking Winifred. As Clare joined the older woman, Winifred gave her a troubled glance.

Clare asked, "How is my uncle?"

"Still unconscious," Winifred said, pausing over her coffee.

"Will the doctor soon be here?"

"I expect so," the dark-haired woman said in her aloof way. Then she added, "I'm sorry I made that scene last night. You and Jeff must realize I was overwrought."

"Of course," Clare said, surprised at the mellowing of the older woman's tone. She had an idea Winifred might not be too sure of her ground and be afraid she'd gone too far. Perhaps she didn't know whether or not her husband had made his will and if Clare had been named as a prominent heir.

Winifred took a sip of her coffee and went on, "Of course I do feel strongly about Benjamin remaining here. I know it to be his wish."

Clare had poured her orange juice, and now she said tactfully, "I think Jeff and I felt it was mainly a matter of care. If Uncle Benjamin required an operation, he would have to go to the hospital for surgery. A hospital has so much equipment not available in a home. While his stroke doesn't seem to call for operating facilities, he still might have better therapy available at a hospital."

The older woman frowned. "If it were a matter of an operation, I would have no choice. But I do in this instance, and so I must abide by what I know were Benjamin's wishes."

Clare sighed. "It's a dreadful thing! He seemed so well yesterday. I only hope he recovers."

Winifred said, "There was no warning at all. I awoke when I heard your screams. Benjamin has had his own bedroom for years so that we don't disturb each other. He has suffered from insomnia and often gets up during the night and reads or does some work until he feels sleepy again. I'm normally a sound sleeper."

"My finding him was part of a macabre experience," Clare confessed. "Someone knocked at my door and called my name again, just as they did the night I was attacked. That is how I happened to go down to the library at that hour."

The older woman's eyes fixed on her piercingly from behind her horn-rimmed glasses. "You were attacked one night and my husband on another. It makes one believe it was the ghost!"

Clare felt uneasy. "There was surely something strange about it," she ventured.

"Benjamin's shock was partially brought on by his fall from the ladder. But what came into the library to cause him to topple to the floor?"

"I guess only he can tell us," Clare said. She was still suspicious of the dark woman.

"And will he ever be able to do that?"

"I hope so," Clare said. "It is only a first stroke. Most people recover from strokes unless they are massive. And many never have another one. I'm hopeful he'll get better."

Winifred pushed her empty cup aside. "I wish I could be as optimistic," she said. "Benjamin has been overdoing for years. I pleaded with him to go easier, but he refused. Now it seems the time of reckoning has come."

"How many nurses will there be?"

"Three. Another one should be arriving soon," Winifred said.

"If there is anything I can do, please tell me," Clare said awkwardly. "I want to help."

"Thank you," the older woman said. She rose from the table. "I'll keep you informed of your uncle's progress. In the meantime, I expect you'll continue to assist Jeff in the library."

"I suppose so," Clare said. "Keeping busy will ease the suspense."

Winifred hesitated at the door on her way out of the dining room. "I'd appreciate it if you'd try to explain my feeling to Jeff. I'm sure I shocked him last night."

"I will," Clare promised.

"Thank you," the dark woman said, and went out.

Clare finished a light breakfast and then went to the library. Jeff was already there and at work checking through a file folder. He turned to greet her, and she saw that his handsome face bore a strained look.

"Good morning," he said.

"Good morning," she answered, crossing over to him. "Did you get in contact with Professor Curtis?"

"I just finished talking to him on the phone a few minutes ago," Jeff said. "He's coming over."

"I hope he is able to talk some sense into Winifred," she said worriedly.

The young librarian grimaced. "I wouldn't be hopeful after that scene she put on for us last night."

"I had breakfast with her, and she sort of apologized," Clare told him.

"Sort of?"

Clare sighed. "She admitted she'd been wrong, but not with much grace. Then she acted as if she were sorry she'd made the admission in the first place."

"That sounds more in character."

"I tried to rationalize about taking Uncle Benjamin to a hospital, but I didn't really get anywhere."

"So things are just the same."

"He's still in a coma."

"The doctor should soon be here," Jeff said. "I'd like to have Professor Curtis here at the same time. He might be able to convince Winifred that the doctor's advice was sound. Your uncle should be in a hospital."

"She still contends he dislikes and distrusts hospitals."

"That's like saying someone dislikes and distrusts the police," Jeff said angrily. "Where else can one go in extreme illness but to a hospital? Benjamin may be up there dying now for lack of professional care."

"She doesn't think so," Clare said, sinking wearily into a chair next to the desk. "And now she's talking about the ghost being responsible for my uncle's condition."

"Did she say that?"

"Yes. She hinted strongly that the curse attached to the Book of Gospels had finally been invoked against Uncle Benjamin."

Jeff's eyes narrowed. "I'm surprised at this sudden change of opinion on her part. Normally she says little about the ghost."

"My guess is she is making use of the legend now."

"It could be," he said, moving toward the wall of books. Then he turned to face her. "I told you that we've had some strange manifestations here: books being moved around and things like that."

"Yes."

"Now I've discovered something else. Some of our valuable books are missing. They've vanished completely."

"Did you tell Uncle Benjamin about this?"

"No. I made a final check this morning. Now I'm certain that at least a dozen of the more valuable books on the shelves have disappeared."

"What about those in the safe?"

"Those are the ones of greatest value," Jeff said. "They're all there. So it would seem that if the books vanish through ghostly hands, the ghost has no power over the locked safe. And that doesn't fit in with any picture of the supernatural I've ever had."

"Would Winifred know which books are the most valuable?" Clare asked.

"I suppose so, at least in a casual way. She's been around Benjamin enough to have some idea."

Clare gave the young man a knowing look. "She hasn't approved of the money Uncle Benjamin has been spending on his collection. Could it be she's taken the books and sold them?"

"I don't know," Jeff said. "In that case she'd have to have a confederate, someone to dispose of them for her. I doubt if she'd know where to get rid of them at a decent price."

Clare got up, seized by an idea. "Suppose Uncle Benjamin found out about her thefts. That may be why he was in the library last night. Did he know you were checking on certain volumes?"

"Yes," Jeff said. "We thought they'd only been displaced; a malicious act on the part of the ghost. But now I know some of the books are gone."

"He might have discovered the same thing. Winifred could have gone into the library on a foraging expedition and been discovered by him. They might have quarreled and his stroke have been the result of the quarrel. Then, to be sure he was found, Winifred played the ghost and led me down there."

Jeff showed interest. "You may have hit on something."

She grimaced. "Don't accept it too easily. It's all based on conjecture."

"That may be the only way we'll find out the truth, now that your uncle is in the state's he's in," Jeff said.

"Let's hope we can get him to a hospital and that he improves."

At that moment they heard the doctor arrive downstairs. They waited tensely for some verdict from him. Jeff hovered by the door of the library so as to be sure to catch the doctor's attention when he came down from the sickroom on the third floor. Clare waited with him, conscious that she was very much concerned about her uncle.

Jeff whispered, "I hear Winifred and the doctor talking. He's coming down in a moment."

A few minutes later the large, bald-headed Dr. Greensmith came down the stairs. Jeff went out to greet him, and Clare followed. The doctor recognized them from the previous night.

"I suppose you're wondering about Mr. Rand's condition," he said.

"That is true," Jeff agreed. "Is he any better?"

"Yes and no," Dr. Greensmith said with a scowl. "I'd be much more certain about everything if I had him in a hospital."

"He hasn't regained consciousness yet, has he?" Clare asked.

"His eyes are open, and I think he's emerged from his coma," the doctor said. "But his mind is still dulled, and he is completely paralyzed, unable to talk or move."

Jeff said, "But there has been a slight improvement?"

"Yes," Dr. Greensmith acknowledged.

"Did he seem to recognize anyone?" Clare asked.

"I'm afraid not," the doctor said. "But then I think it is too soon for that. He's shown some progress in the last few hours. It could be that he'll improve dramatically between now and tomorrow."

"When will you be back?" Jeff asked.

"I'll try to come tonight," the doctor said. "Or I can be reached any time, if he seems to be definitely worse."

Clare asked, "Has his wife given in about his being taken to a hospital?"

"I'm afraid not," Dr. Greensmith said with a sigh. "Perhaps later, when she is not so frightened, she'll see reason. It's hard to say."

Jeff said, "A close friend of Mr. Rand's is coming to visit us this morning. I'm hoping he may be able to put some sense into her head."

"I'd like to see it happen," the doctor said. "With proper care, there is a strong possibility Mr. Rand might recover. I'm having difficulty hiring a night nurse. If I can't get one, I'm not sure what I'll do."

"Can I help?" Clare asked. "I've had training as a nurse's aide. I did voluntary work at a hospital in Chicago."

Dr. Greensmith showed interest. "It may be I'll have to call on you for help for a night or two.

I could put you in direct telephone contact with a qualified nurse working in this area. In an emergency, she could rush over here for a few minutes."

Clare began to feel uneasy, but she didn't want to withdraw her offer. "I'll do it if you think I've had adequate experience."

"There's very little to be done for your uncle except watch him and see that he's comfortable," Dr. Greensmith said. "I'd say your training is adequate for that, especially with a regular nurse to call on."

Jeff said, "You can let us know."

"I will," the doctor promised. "It would be the night shift from eleven to seven. That is the difficult one."

Jeff saw the doctor out and then came back to join Clare in the library. The young man looked concerned.

"Do you think you should have offered to take on that nursing chore?" he asked.

"I didn't like just to stand by when I've had some experience," she said.

"You're right," he agreed. "I'd be just as happy if you weren't called on. It's a heavy responsibility, in spite of what the doctor says. And with Winifred in her present mood, she'd enjoy nothing more than blaming you if anything happened."

"I realize that." Clare sighed. "Perhaps before tonight she'll change her mind about Uncle Benjamin going to a hospital."

Jeff looked gloomy. "Don't count on that," he warned her.

The doorbell rang again, and this time it was Professor Alan Curtis. Mrs. Fox ushered the energetic professor in, and he at once rushed up to the landing on the second floor where Jeff was waiting for him. Distress showed on his round face.

"What dreadful news about Benjamin," he said. "May I go up and see him for a moment?"

"You can try," Jeff said. "I'm not certain whether or not his wife is allowing him any visitors. He's still in a bad state."

"I'll see what she has to say," Professor Curtis said. "I'll be back down in a few minutes." And he vanished up the stairway leading to the third floor bedrooms.

Jeff came back into the library and said, "We'll see how he makes out with Winifred."

"Has she been favorably disposed to him in the past?" Clare asked.

Jeff shrugged and stared out of the window. "Sometimes she has, and at other times she's stormed about his talking your uncle into giving him the bulk of his books. She feels the collection should be auctioned at your uncle's death and the money put into the estate."

"I think it ought to be Uncle Benjamin's decision," she said.

"So do I," Jeff agreed. "But that's been her attitude."

Clare gazed at the opposite sidewalk. "I don't see any sign of our friend with the dark glasses today."

"We have trouble enough without him," Jeff said bitterly.

Before she could make any reply, Professor Alan Curtis came into the library to join them. His round face wore a troubled expression, and he eyed them dolefully.

"Benjamin didn't recognize me," he said in a stunned tone. "Most distressing! I spoke to him, and there was not a sign that he knew me."

"The doctor said he was still in a state of mental confusion," Clare told him.

"I was only there a moment," the professor went on. "Winifred hesitated about allowing me to see him at all. But she did allow me a short visit."

Jeff said, "I hope you expressed surprise that he wasn't in a hospital."

"As a matter of fact, I did," the professor said with a slight frown. "Why has she kept him here?"

"A stubborn notion on her part," Clare said. "We begged her to send him to a hospital."

"Extraordinary!" Professor Alan Curtis said in his expressive fashion.

"It might help if you suggested he be put in a hospital," Jeff said. "We've been waiting for you to come and put your weight behind this."

The professor sighed. "I very much fear it wouldn't do any good. She's made up her mind, and she won't change it. At least that's the impression I received."

"I think you've gotten the correct one," Clare said.

The round face of the professor showed concern. "Now do tell me just how it all happened. I know none of the details."

Jeff said, "Clare was the one who discovered him. Perhaps she should tell you."

"Please do," the professor said, turning to her.

Clare proceeded to give him a full account of what had taken place. When she finished, she said, "Winifred seems to believe it was the ghost who struck him down."

Professor Curtis looked awed. He sank down into a nearby chair and in a taut voice said, "Of course! The Nun of Valencia!"

Jeff said, "I find her too ready to believe it.

Blaming the ghost is a convenient way of taking any blame from the living."

The professor stared at him in surprise. "But we both know the dark history of the Book of Gospels. It's no secret that violent deaths have been the fate of most of its previous owners."

"It doesn't have to be true in this case."

"Benjamin didn't take the curse lightly," the professor reminded them.

"A lot of odd things have been happening here," Jeff went on. "And some of the valuable books have vanished."

The professor showed alarm. "Have you done anything about this?"

"No. I only just discovered the losses," Jeff said.

"I think you should talk to the police if the books don't turn up," Professor Curtis said. "You could have a thief to deal with."

"If so, the thief would have to be someone in the house," Jeff pointed out. "The most likely suspect is Winifred. And this seems a poor time to turn the police on her. Benjamin needs her."

"Undoubtedly," the professor said, his round face troubled. "So you'll simply have to wait until Benjamin's condition shows improvement."

"If it does," Jeff said.

"That is something to consider," the professor agreed. "It may be that all these things are tied up somehow; that they are all part of the curse."

Clare said, "There's a strange-looking gray-haired man with dark glasses living next door. He's been standing outside the house, staring up at our windows."

Professor Curtis looked shocked. "Now why should he be doing that?"

"That's what we'd like to know," Jeff said grimly.

"He has some interest in what's going on here," Clare said. "Why I can't say."

Professor Curtis stood up. "Well, we must hope for Benjamin's recovery. Then he may be able to straighten us all out as to what happened."

Jeff said, "I think it's important you keep in touch with us."

"I shall," the professor said. "And I'll speak to Winifred before I leave about the advisability of placing poor Benjamin in a hospital."

"Please do that," Jeff begged him.

"I will," the Professor promised him. Then he turned to Clare and in a solemn voice warned her, "From this point on you must take particular care. You are the only blood relation of Benjamin's in the house. And if the Nun of Valencia is out for revenge, you're the next one likely to be struck down."

CHAPTER EIGHT

Professor Curtis left shortly after giving Clare the warning, but the grim threat of his words remained with her all through the long and trying day.

When dinner time came, Winifred sought out Clare and told her, "I want you to go to Pierre's for dinner as usual."

"What about you?" Clare asked.

"I may join you later," her uncle's wife said rather evasively. "Benjamin showed a bit more of a response a few minutes ago, and I don't want to leave him just yet."

"I can wait a little," Clare said. "I'm not hungry."

"You need nourishment," Winifred said. "I'd prefer that you go now."

"I could have dinner with Jeff," Clare suggested. "He goes to a restaurant on Charles Street."

"No," the older woman said. "I'd prefer you to go to Pierre's. Then if I decide to join you, I won't have to eat alone."

"Very well," Clare agreed. And so, a quarter of an hour later, she found herself seated at a table in the restaurant next door. Pierre showed her to a table and expressed his regrets about her uncle's illness.

Shortly afterward, as Clare was starting her soup, Madame Reaux came out from the kitchen to speak to her. The melancholy Frenchwoman said, "I have just heard about *Monsieur* Rand. It is too bad!"

"Thank you," Clare said.

"Is he in pain?" the woman asked.

"I think not."

"That is a small blessing," the proprietress of the restaurant said. "Please let us know his condition from day to day."

"I will," Clare said. "Dr. Greensmith hopes he may recover. And I know nothing would make him happier than to be here having dinner at your fine restaurant."

"Thank you, *mademoiselle,*" the woman said. "You are then his true niece?"

"Yes. He and my father were brothers."

"How fortunate that you arrived before this happened," the Frenchwoman said. "Your uncle must have taken great joy in having you here. He has no children of his own, has he?"

"No."

"Then he would regard you in the same light as a daughter."

"I hope he did." Clare sighed. "I am very fond of him. I didn't realize how much I cared for him until this happened."

"I understand," the woman sympathized. "It takes a great tragedy for one fully to understand one's feelings."

"That is very true," Clare agreed.

"Your uncle will be constantly in my thoughts,

and so will you and his good wife," Madame Reaux told her before returning to the kitchen.

Clare was touched by the Frenchwoman's sympathetic interest. She lingered over her meal in the hope that Winifred might join her, but she didn't.

As she was about ready to leave, Clare glanced across to the other side of the intimate restaurant and saw a familiar face. At a small table, similar to the one where she sat, was seated the odd-looking gray-haired man with the dark glasses. He seemed to be paying no attention to her, but she had the weird feeling that he had been spying on her as she ate.

His presence in the restaurant made her nervous. She knew it was ridiculous to be afraid of this stranger whom she'd seen only a few times before and who had a perfect right to be there. But she was afraid. She couldn't say why. It seemed that an aura of evil somehow hung over him. From the moment she'd seen him gazing up at the library windows, she'd felt he presented some kind of menace.

She signed her check, as she'd been taught by her uncle. The restaurant sent him a monthly bill. Then she quickly got up and walked out, being careful to avoid looking in the direction of the man with the dark glasses as she went by his table. When she reached the cool air of the foggy night, she stood for a moment and breathed it in with relief.

She'd been in the house all day, and it had been a time of tension. She longed to stroll in the darkness to break the mood of depression she was in and work off some of her tension. She decided to stroll up the street in the direction of Boston Common. Mount Vernon Street was not well lighted as Charles Street was. It was mostly residential.

Even at that early hour in the evening, there were few people on the sidewalk. She walked along at a good pace, preoccupied with her own troubled thoughts. And then, as she reached the top of the hill, she had a strange feeling that she was being followed! For a moment or two she didn't dare to look around. And then, mustering her courage, she did—and received a nasty shock!

Not more than a half-dozen yards behind her was the man with the dark glasses. She recognized his shabby black coat and gray hat as well as the glasses. Her heart pounded more rapidly, and she increased her pace. Her ears caught the sound of his distant footsteps as he also began to move faster. This sent her into a panic.

She was on the other side of the hill and in sight of the Boston Common. Not far ahead was the intersection of Tremont Street and the Common. It would be busy there, and she would be safe. She practically ran down the hill in the direction of Beacon Street.

As she raced ahead, her face distorted by fear, she heard the man with the dark glasses hurrying to overtake her. She ran out into the street and directly in the path of an oncoming taxi. The taxi came to a tire-screeching halt just in time to avoid running her down.

The irate driver leaned out and demanded, "Are you crazy?"

"I'm sorry," she faltered, standing in the gleam of the headlights. "Have you a passenger?"

"No. And it's lucky! Stopping like that, I'd have sent him out through the windshield," the driver complained.

She moved back to the rear door and opened it.

"I need a cab badly," she said. And she got inside.

The driver was still fuming. "You gave me a nasty scare, miss," he said.

"I know I was stupid," she told him, glancing out into the darkness in search of her pursuer. There he was—standing on the corner of the street, glaring at the cab in frustrated anger.

The cabby said, "Where to?"

"Mount Vernon Street," she said, giving him the number.

"You're not a block away," the cabby said suspiciously. "I'll have to drive all around to get you there. The simplest way would be to walk back down the hill."

"I can't do that," she said desperately. Quickly contriving a story, she went on, "I've had a fight with my boy friend. He's on the corner waiting for me!"

The cabby gave her a bleak glance over his shoulder. "So that's it!"

"You do understand?"

"Sure," he said. "I've had my own troubles with my missus. But I never tried to get myself run down."

"Please drive on," she said nervously. "He might try to come over to the cab and make a scene." It had just occurred to her that if she could make up a story, so could the man with the dark glasses. He could get in the cab, pretending to be her husband, and perhaps use a weapon to force her to go along with him in his lie. She could wind up his prisoner despite the sanctuary of the cab.

"Okay, miss," the cabby said, driving on. "I know how these things are."

She sat trembling in the near-darkness of the cab as they skirted the area on the journey back to Mount Vernon Street. When they reached the entrance to the red brick house, there was no sign of the man with dark glasses. She paid the cabby her fare and a generous tip. Then she got out and hurried up the stairs and into the house.

She was grateful to find that Jeff had returned from dinner and was in the library, working. She rushed over to his desk and breathlessly told him, "I've just had a terrible experience."

He got up. "What now?"

She explained. "If I hadn't almost been hit by that cab, I'm sure he'd have caught up with me."

Jeff showed concern. "Why would he follow you?"

"I don't know."

"Maybe he was just walking in the same direction."

"No," she protested. "He was following me. I could tell. And he waited and watched from the curb when I got into the cab."

Jeff said, "Then he has to be interested in what is going on here in some way."

"I'm sure of that. Remember how he stared up at the windows?"

"I said he was staring at you," Jeff reminded her.

She crimsoned. "I remember."

"He may be some kind of sex maniac," Jeff said. "I don't like it at all."

"I'm terrified. I won't dare go walking alone after dark again."

"Not even in the daytime," the young librarian warned her. "In a city like this, it's not unknown for people to be abducted in daylight on a busy street."

"Now you're really frightening me," she worried.

"We may as well face facts," Jeff told her. "This

oddball next door has some sinister interest in you. You'll do well to keep out of his way."

"I wonder that Madame Reaux would rent her apartment to anyone like that," she said.

"He may behave perfectly normally as far as she's concerned."

"I don't suppose it would do any good to tell her or ask her more about him."

"I doubt it," Jeff said. "She probably only knows what he has told her, and that wouldn't be much. Better to keep to the house unless one of us is with you."

"I will," she said. "I wouldn't have gone to Pierre's tonight except that Winifred suggested it. She said she might join me. But she didn't."

Jeff's eyebrows rose. "Winifred suggested it?"

"Yes."

"That could mean something," he said. "Maybe she deliberately sent you there so harm would come to you."

Clare glanced apprehensively toward the open library door to be sure the older woman wasn't anywhere nearby. Then in a low voice she asked him, "Do you think she might have done that?"

"It's possible. Perhaps he's her fellow conspirator. He may be the one acting as a fence for the stolen books, assuming that she has been taking them."

She gasped. "I never thought of that."

"Maybe your uncle found it out, and that brought on the stroke."

"How can we discover if Winifred knows this man?"

"By careful watching and waiting," Jeff said. "You can be sure she'll never admit knowing him."

Clare slumped down into a chair and looked at

him despondently. "If anything happens to Uncle Benjamin, I'm leaving here at once. I can't stand the atmosphere of brooding evil."

Jeff said, "You'll never be happy if you run away."

"I may not live if I stay here too long," she protested.

"I don't think it's that bad," he consoled her. "Otherwise I wouldn't encourage you to remain. You know how I feel about you."

"How we feel about each other is unimportant right now," she said wearily. "The big problem is how to survive this ordeal."

"Take it twenty-four hours at a time," was his advice. "I'm trying to calm my nerves by keeping busy. This is a rare book your uncle recently purchased from Goodspeed's, a first edition of Shelley's *Adonais*. There are only a few in existence."

She eyed the slender volume with interest. "Shouldn't that be in the safe?"

"I'm putting it there when I finish going over it," he said. "There's a strange story connected with the *Adonais*. A printer named William Hoyt was a passionate collector of Shelleyana. He longed to own a first edition of this book, but none ever came his way. So he gathered the proper type, paper and other materials and made a very clever forgery of the book. But it wasn't good enough to fool his friends, who were experts in the field. They said nothing, in consideration of his feelings, and he became obsessed with the idea that the fake he'd contrived was real. He died believing it. The odd ending to the story is that the Hoyt forgery, being the only one in existence, became a collector's item in its own right and commanded a high price from the museum which purchased it."

She said, "You take the same interest in books as my uncle."

"I suppose I do," he agreed.

"There's nothing wrong with that," she hastened to say. "I'm sure I could easily grow to have the same feeling for them myself."

"That's one of the reasons Benjamin became so fond of you."

"Poor Uncle Benjamin! Do you suppose we'll ever all sit down and talk together again?"

"We can hope so," Jeff said, studying her sympathetically. "I hope he regains his health and is able to instruct you in the care and feeding of books. You'll learn to take a book off a shelf, weigh it in your hand and really look at it. You'll note whether the cover is cloth or leather and if the lettering is gilt, red or black; whether it is a large book, medium-sized or small. The terms folio, quarto, octavo and duodecimo will all come to have meaning to you. You'll begin to check the title page for the copyright date and the edition of the book. Then you'll evaluate the illustrations, if there are any, and check their clarity. Soon this will become second nature to you, and you'll be started as a book specialist."

"It seems a long way off at this minute," she said.

"Let's hope it's not."

She got up from the chair and was about to go upstairs when Winifred appeared in the doorway of the room. The dark-haired woman looked weary.

She asked, "I'm not interrupting you, am I?"

"No," Jeff said. "Come in."

Winifred approached Clare. "Dr. Greensmith just called. He hasn't been able to get a night nurse, and he wants you to sit with your uncle through the night. Do you mind?"

Clare felt a surge of nerves again but said, "I told him I would."

"That's what he explained to me," Winifred said. "I had no idea you trained as a nurse."

"A nurse's aide," Clare corrected the older woman. "It's quite different."

"At any rate, he seems to think you can do the job," the older woman said. "And he left a number you can call if you need aid. It's the number of a house in the area where he has a regular nurse on duty."

Clare nodded. "He said he'd do that."

Winifred was studying her sharply. "You seem nervous about it. Do you want to do it?"

"Oh, yes," Clare said. "I'm a little nervous, but I'll probably manage well enough."

"Dr. Greensmith has made every effort, but he can't get a nurse for the night shift," Winifred said. "I can't understand why. I should think there'd be some available."

Jeff spoke up. "Nurses are in very short supply."

"I had no idea," Winifred said.

"That is one of the reasons I've felt Benjamin should be in a hospital," Jeff went on.

The dark-haired woman's face took on that familiar cold expression. "There's no need to discuss that further. I have made up my mind. Benjamin stays here. He's doing very well. I'm sure he recognized me a few minutes ago."

Jeff said, "May I go up and see him?"

Winifred hesitated. Then she said, "Yes. But don't stay more than a minute or two. We mustn't strain him."

"I won't," he said.

Winifred turned to Clare. "Then I'll tell the nurse on duty now you'll be taking over at eleven."

"Yes," Clare said.

"I'm grateful for this," Winifred told her, and left them.

Jeff waited until the dark-haired woman had gone before he gave a deep sigh and said, "Well, it looks as if you're in for it."

"I expected to be," she told him. "I'd better go up to my room and get some rest before I begin my vigil."

"Would you like me to sit with you?"

"No. That might worry Uncle Benjamin."

He frowned. "You could be right. I'm going up to have a look at him now. Why don't you come along on your way up to your room?"

It seemed a reasonable idea. She said, "All right."

They quietly made their way up to the sickroom. The door was partly open, and the room was softly lighted by a single lamp on a dresser. The elderly nurse on duty was standing by the bed, gazing at her patient.

When they went in, the nurse turned to them and nodded. She made a motion for them to be quiet. They approached the bedside, and Clare saw that Benjamin's eyes were closed and he seemed to be resting. She and Jeff stood there for a couple of minutes and then went out.

Jeff mounted the stairs to the fourth floor with her and asked her, "What did you think?"

"He seemed to be breathing very easily and sleeping," she said.

"I guess that's a good sign," he agreed worriedly. "I was hoping his eyes would be open and he might recognize me."

"That was asking too much."

"I guess you're right," he agreed.

"Maybe in the morning he'll be better," she said.

"I don't see him improving much unless Winifred lets him go to a hospital," Jeff worried.

They reached the dark fourth floor, and Jeff saw her to her door. "Try to get some sleep before you go down there," he advised.

"I'm going to."

He sighed. "I'm worried about you being there alone. I can join you if you like."

"No," she said. "If I want you, I'll know you're not far away. I can always come up here for you."

"Don't hesitate to do that," he urged her.

"I won't," she promised.

"And remember I love you," he told her gently, and held her in his arms for a brief kiss.

She went into her room, set her clock to go off at ten-thirty and stretched out on the bed to get an hour and a half's sleep. She slept for only a few minutes. But she did get some rest. She was awake when the alarm sounded. She got up quickly and turned it off, then took a shower and changed into a plain linen dress which was the closest thing she had to a uniform.

At about ten to eleven, she went downstairs and took over from the elderly nurse. The nurse told her in a low voice, "Mrs. Rand has gone to bed. I don't believe you'll have any trouble with him. He's still asleep."

Clare looked and saw this was so. "He seems comfortable," she said.

"He is," the elderly nurse agreed.

Clare said, "Do you think he has a good chance to get better?"

The nurse nodded. "Yes. I've attended patients worse off than he who have recovered from strokes."

Clare said good night to the nurse and took the chair by her uncle's bedside. She had brought a magazine with her, and she began to read. It made her drowsy, and soon she was sound asleep.

She didn't know how long she slept, but when she came awake with a start she was engulfed by a feeling of guilt. She had let down herself and her patient. And then she received a surprise. Her uncle had awakened and was staring at her. She was sure of it. His eyes seemed to be fixed on her.

She said, "Uncle Benjamin!" and bent close to him.

She had hoped that he might try to say her name. But she was to be disappointed. He seemed to shift his gaze, and now he was staring up over her shoulder, staring at some point behind her. And in his eyes there was a look of sheer horror! It made her flesh creep, and she found herself too frightened to turn and study the shadowy room behind her.

CHAPTER NINE

Finally Clare forced herself to turn and look in the dark shadows of the room behind her.

And she saw the phantom—the avenging Nun of Valencia, just as she had been described. The shadowy gray figure in the nun's habit had a bony hand upraised, and in the hand was a knife with a glistening blade—a knife destined to be plunged into Clare!

She did not dare scream, with her uncle so ill beside her. But she jumped up from her chair and stumbled toward the doorway. As she did so, the figure of the phantom came after her. Fear gave Clare wings, and she raced down the corridor and up the stairs to the fourth floor without glancing behind her again.

Going directly to Jeff's door, she banged on it and cried his name. Then she tried the knob, and the door opened. She entered his room just as he sprang out of bed. He came hurrying toward her.

"What is it?"

"The phantom!"

"Where?"

"In my uncle's room!"

He shoved her aside and was already on his way

downstairs. She gave him a warning, calling to him about the knife. But she was certain he had gotten too far on his way to hear her. She followed him quickly.

When she caught up with him, he was standing in the middle of her uncle's room. She hesitantly went to the door and stared into the room. There was no sign of the phantom. She felt sick and weary.

Jeff came back out of the room to stand before her in the hall. "There's no sign of a ghost or human in there," he said.

"The phantom was there—the Nun of Valencia! She had a knife and was ready to stab me with it!"

Jeff looked grim. "Well, she's not here now!"

"I know that," she said dispiritedly.

He was looking at her was frank disbelief. "I think you must have fallen asleep."

"I did go to sleep," she admitted. "And it was when I woke up that I saw her."

"You dreamed it!"

"No!" she protested.

"Don't be too sure," Jeff warned her. "Often dreams can seem terribly real."

She looked up into his handsome face and, with urgency in her tone, said, "Uncle Benjamin was awake, too. And he saw the ghost. It was the fear in his eyes which alerted me. Look at him now. He probably is frightened to death, poor dear!"

Jeff gave her a doubting look. "I'll bet he's asleep."

"I don't think so," she said.

Reluctantly Jeff went back into the room, and she accompanied him. They went to the bedside of the paralyzed man, and Clare was proven right. He was still awake, and there was a look of terror in his eyes which could not be denied.

She glanced at Jeff. "Now what do you say?"

Jeff was frowning. "He does look frightened."

"I told you," she said.

Jeff leaned toward the man who had been his mentor and idol and in a low, reassuring voice said, "It's all right. You don't need to be afraid for yourself or Clare. I'll be close by."

Benjamin Rand's eyes seemed to lose some of their sick terror. But he was a prisoner of his body and in no way could give them any sign that he understood. They stood by him for a moment or two longer, and then Jeff touched Clare's arm and led her out into the hall again.

She said, "What now?"

"You can go on staying by his bedside the rest of the night," Jeff told her. "I'll get a chair and sit in the hallway outside the door."

"That's not fair to you!"

"I can't let you remain here alone."

"I could wake Mrs. Fox or Winifred."

"And start another lot of recriminations," he said with disgust. "I'd rather do it this way."

She looked up at him anxiously. "You know the phantom was in there! You saw the look in my uncle's eyes!"

He sighed. "I guess he must have seen something."

"He saw her. The Nun."

Jeff said, "We'll talk about it in the morning. You go in to him now."

"All right," she said. And she went back into the room and sat down in the chair again. Her Uncle Benjamin's eyes were still open, and now they were fixed on her with a look of solemn concern. She reached out and patted one of his hands. "You don't need to worry," she consoled him. "Try to rest."

Not long afterward he closed his eyes, and she could tell he was sleeping. Her long, lonely vigil continued. She did not sleep again. At last seven o'clock came, and the morning nurse arrived.

The young woman said, "The patient seems to be resting well. I'd judge that he had a good night."

"I think so," Clare said, making no mention of her own experience. She guessed that Jeff had discreetly vanished when he heard Mrs. Fox let the nurse in the front door.

The nurse was staring at her. "You look very weary. You should go to bed and get some rest."

"I must," she agreed. "I may be needed again tonight."

The nurse nodded. "I know Dr. Greensmith had no luck getting anyone last night."

Clare left the sickroom and went on up to her own bedroom. There she drew the drapes, hastily undressed and got into bed. She'd been too weary even to think about breakfast. In a few minutes she'd fallen into a deep, exhausted sleep which lasted until the early afternoon.

She awoke feeling starved and anxious to talk to Jeff. After a hurried shower, she dressed and went down to the library. It was empty, so she continued on down to the dining room. She met Mrs. Fox in the hallway.

"You'll be wanting something to eat," the housekeeper said in a tone that suggested she didn't approve of irregular meals.

"I am hungry," Clare said. "But I don't need anything fancy."

"I'll cook some hamburger," Mrs. Fox announced. "Go into the dining room, and I'll bring you some juice and rolls while I'm getting the meat ready."

"Thank you," Clare said. "Where is everyone?"

"Mr. Carney and Mrs. Rand are both out," the housekeeper said in her stiff fashion. "I believe Mr. Carney went to the bank, and Mrs. Rand had some sort of errand to do."

"I see," Clare said, wondering what sort of errand had taken Winifred out. Perhaps it had something to do with stolen books, or maybe the phantom. She had visions of Winifred pretending to be the phantom in order to terrify her and the helpless Benjamin.

"I've just taken up a noon snack for the day nurse," Mrs. Fox said.

"How is my uncle?" she asked.

"The nurse thinks he is much improved. So does Mrs. Rand. He seems to know what is going on in the room, but he can't move or say anything yet."

"Perhaps that will come soon."

"Yes," Mrs. Fox said, and headed in the direction of the kitchen.

As Clare had her first food since the previous evening, she went over all the events of the night in her mind. And the more she thought about it, the more certain she was that it had been Winifred who had come into the room to threaten her, dressed as a ghost. She couldn't prove it yet, but she felt she had to be right.

She had just finished her coffee when Mrs. Fox came into the room and told her, "You're wanted on the phone."

"Do you know who it is?" she asked, getting up from the dining room table.

"It's that Professor Curtis from the university," the housekeeper said.

"Oh, yes," Clare said. "I'll take the call." She went to the nearest extension in the foyer and picked up the phone. "Clare speaking," she told the man at the other end of the line.

"Clare, my dear girl," Professor Curtis said in his usual bubbly fashion, "I do hope I haven't bothered you."

"No. I've just finished lunch," she said. "I played nurse to Uncle Benjamin last night, and I got up only an hour ago."

"How is he?"

"Better."

"Is he able to communicate at all yet?"

"No."

"How dreadful for him," the professor said.

"Some strange things have been happening," she told him, anxious to confide in someone.

"Really?" The professor sounded interested.

"Yes. I'm terrified by some of them."

"That is dreadful. Tell me about it," he urged her.

"I don't dare," she said. "Not over the phone."

There was a short silence at the other end of the line. Then Professor Alan Curtis asked her, "Do these frightening things have anything to do with Benjamin?"

"Yes."

"Dear, dear," the professor sputtered. "I'd like to come over and closet myself with you and hear all the details, but unhappily I can't leave my office today. I'm expecting a screen person from Hollywood. One of my collectees. She'll have a fit if I'm not on hand to greet her."

"What time is she arriving?"

"That is the thing," he lamented. "One never knows. To give you an idea of the kind of neurotic she is, she wired and had me reserve a suite of two rooms for her at the Ritz: one room for her and the other for her stuffed leopard. Now I ask you, is that sane?"

She laughed wryly. "Not very."

"Well, the thing is: she may arrive any time with or without the stuffed leopard. We're to have a discussion about some of her more indiscreet letters, which she left with me in a mood of blatant emotional distress and which she now feels she should have back. I, on the other hand, prize them as the spice of her collection and am determined they shall not leave Bedford University's sacred archives."

"You seem to have enough dilemmas of your own without mine," she said.

"That is not true," the professor said. "I do want to talk with you. I have an idea the screen person won't be here for hours, so why don't you quickly call a taxi and come over and meet me at my office here at the university?"

She hesitated. It was a tempting offer. She badly wanted to unburden herself to someone. Yet Jeff had warned her not to leave the house alone. However, it seemed that she would be safe enough if she had a taxi pick her up and take her to the university and also returned in a cab.

So she said, "All right. I'll call a taxi and be there as soon as I can."

"Wonderful," Professor Curtis said in his enthusiastic fashion. "Then I shall be seeing you soon."

As soon as she finished talking with him, she phoned the taxi service. Then she went to the kitchen and told Mrs. Fox she was going out for a little while.

"If Mr. Carney returns before I do, tell him I've gone to the university," she said.

Mrs. Fox nodded in her curt fashion. "Yes, miss."

Clare then went upstairs to the sickroom. Her uncle was asleep, and the nurse came out to her. She told the nurse where she was going and inquired about her uncle's condition. He was much the same as when she'd left.

She went down to the steps, and the taxi arrived after a short wait. She gave him the address of the university on Commonwealth Avenue and was on her way. The drive took less time than she had expected. She left the taxi at the entrance of the university library building, which were huge, mostly concrete and glass in plain square designs.

Entering the reception area, she mentioned Professor Curtis' address and was directed to an elevator in the left corridor of the big building. Within a few minutes she was whisked to the fourth floor where the special collection department was located. Here the atmosphere was very literary, in spite of the modern design of the area. She was greeted by another young female receptionist, who took her name and vanished through a doorway to the left.

Clare passed the time studying a display case given to books and other items related to the famed humorist, Mark Twain. She was reading the various cards attached to the exhibits when the girl returned and told her Professor Curtis was waiting to see her.

Following the girl down a short corridor, Clare found herself ushered into a spacious office with a high ceiling. In one corner of the office a smiling Professor Alan Curtis stood at his desk. The walls of the room were decorated with memorabilia of famous writers and actors.

Professor Alan Curtis advanced to her and took

her hand in his. "What a delicious privilege to have you here. This is my simple workshop."

She gazed about her in admiration. "I don't find it that simple. It's terribly impressive."

The professor directed his cigarette holder to a large oil painting of a cinema star on the far wall. "That is the dear lady I'm waiting for. Sitting here with her as I do every day, I feel she's continually in the room with me."

"It is life-size," Clare agreed, studying the large portrait.

"Life-size and glaring," the professor sighed, "and in that respect entirely like the good lady herself. Do sit down. And I'm going to take a chair by you. I want to hear all about last night."

"It was frightening, not only for me but also for my uncle," she said, sitting in the pre-offered chair.

Professor Curtis was in the chair beside her, his body turned toward her, his hand on the chair arm as he gazed at her with a searching look on his round face. "Do tell me all about it," he insisted.

She sighed and began a recital of the previous night's events.

Professor Curtis sighed. "From all you have said, I'd expect the intruder was the Nun of Valencia. You have heard about her wreaking vengeance on the various owners of the Book of Gospels."

"Yes. But I could not believe the legend."

"Do you now?"

"I'm closer to accepting it," she admitted.

The professor's brow was furrowed. "From what you say, it is probable that your uncle recognized the ghost."

"His eyes showed terror."

"As they undoubtedly would in such a crisis. He has feared the vengeance of that phantom for some time."

"I've heard that."

"It's true," the professor said. "When you returned with Jeff Carney, there was no sign of the ghost?"

"No."

"Well, ghosts can vanish at will. But you say your uncle still revealed fear in his eyes."

Professor Alan Curtis rose and began to pace. "I'm of the opinion it was the ghost and that your uncle recognized it."

"It would almost seem so," Clare agreed.

"Everything points to it," Benjamin's friend declared. "I'm sure she also visited him earlier, and that is when he had the stroke."

"You think the sight of her that other time brought on his condition?"

"The Nun of Valencia avenged herself on him by making him fall from the ladder and bringing on the paralysis."

"If that was what happened, it is understandable that he should be terrified of her," Clare observed.

The professor nodded gravely. "He is familiar with the legend, and he knew what the visitations meant. You will remember that I warned you that you could be the next victim."

"Yes, you did say that."

He made a sweeping dramatic gesture with the hand holding the cigarette holder. "And you have discovered that I was right."

"You were," she agreed.

The professor studied her with serious eyes. "You have seen her, and you will recognize her when she comes after you again."

She registered alarm. "You think I may expect another attempt on my life?"

"Yes," he said. "The attacks will go on as long as your uncle keeps the Book of Gospels in his possession."

"But there's nothing he can do about the book in his present condition," she said. "Why should the phantom continue to harass us?"

Professor Alan Curtis looked solemn. "That is the way it has always been. In the past, the Nun of Valencia has extracted vengeance on entire families, merely because the head of the households owned that cursed manuscript."

"Uncle should never have bought it."

The round-faced man raised his hands in a gesture of resignation. "You must know by now what book collectors can be like. They lose all touch with reality. The desire for a certain volume can outweigh their normal judgment."

She said, "You know it all so well."

"It is a strange world," the professor said. "The experiences one has are quite unique. And many odd things go to make a volume more valuable. As an example, I would guess that in spite of the vicious history of the Book of Gospels and the fate which befell most of its previous owners, it is more prized by collectors than it would be if there were no legend of the avenging Nun of Valencia associated with it."

"So Uncle Benjamin may have been attracted to the manuscript because of its strange history?"

"Exactly," the professor said. "Let me give you a personal example. I have recently purchased a rather commonplace set of Shakespeare's dramatic works, whose value was enhanced by the fact they were a gift of John Severn to the poet John Keats. The set, of small value when it was given to Keats, has actually become a high-priced item because Keats showed his great admiration of Shakespeare's talents by annotating the margins profusely in his own script."

She said, "I can see that, despite the dangers, Uncle Benjamin wanted the Book of Gospels."

"I tried to dissuade him, but it did no good," Professor Curtis said. "And I promise you I wouldn't have the book in the university collection if your uncle gave it to us."

"You'd be afraid?"

"I would. I'd expect to be the first to be struck down."

Clare gave a deep sigh. "I keep thinking it may not be the ghost, but someone pretending to be her."

"Who would carry on such a charade?"

"Winifred or Mrs. Fox," she suggested.

"I don't think either of those good ladies has the imagination for it," he said.

"Perhaps not."

"Stay with the supposition you are dealing with a ghost and you will be a lot safer," he suggested.

"There is something else," she said. "A weird old man with dark glasses has been watching the house and following me. Jeff thinks he may be some kind of madman whose attention I've attracted. Or maybe he is someone working with Winifred to sell some of my uncle's books on the black market. I don't think Jeff has told you, but he has discovered quite a few valuable books are missing."

Professor Alan Curtis listened with a shocked expression on his round face. "Indeed he didn't tell me that," he said. "And I can understand why. Those books have been willed to the library, and it is almost as if they were being stolen from us."

"Do you really feel that way?"

"I do," the professor said. "And I also think you are too quick to blame Winifred for that sort of conspiracy. I can't see her involved in such a scheme."

"Who then?" she asked.

Professor Alan Curtis gave her a knowing look and said, "Has it not occurred to you that the thief in this case could well be Jeff himself?"

CHAPTER TEN

Clare was so stunned by his words that she sat there frozen for a moment. Then she gasped, "You can't mean it!"

"But I do!"

Clare got to her feet. "Jeff would be the last person I'd suspect! You may as well know that we're in love!"

"How touching!" the round-faced professor said without any enthusiasm. "But we must not allow romance to obscure our good judgment, must we?"

She was still incredulous. "You're accusing Jeff of stealing the missing books from my uncle's library?"

He regarded her with frustrating calmness. "I'm merely telling you that I believe it is possible."

"You are supposed to be Jeff's friend!"

He raised a protesting hand. "I am his friend. But it is also evident to me that, with your uncle afflicted by his stroke, Jeff has full command of the library. He could easily steal those books, much more easily than anyone else, and he would also know where to dispose of them for the best price."

She listened, slowly realizing there was a deadly

logic in what he was saying. Jeff was in the best spot to take the books and blame the theft on someone else. But she simply didn't think the young man she loved could be guilty of such a thing.

She said, "Jeff would never steal anything!"

Professor Alan Curtis looked wise. "That is a dangerously broad statement. Let me limit it. I say, Jeff would never steal anything except a book!"

She felt a vague uneasiness. A belief was forming in her mind that Professor Curtis knew something about Jeff's past of which she was unaware.

"You must have some reason for saying that," she told him.

"I have."

"Go on."

The professor toyed with his cigarette lighter as if reluctant to go on. "I find this very painful, my dear. Please remember that it was you who brought up this matter of the book thefts."

"Yes."

He cleared his throat. "As you must know, Jeff worked for several universities before taking this position with your uncle. In fact, his last university post was here at Bedford."

"I know all that."

"Yes," he said. "But what I'm sure you don't know is that two valuable books disappeared from our collection during the period when Jeff was my assistant. I tried to find some suitable explanation without blaming him, but I couldn't."

It was the sort of revelation she'd feared. In a shocked tone she said, "You think he stole books from the university?"

"Only he and I had access to the particular volumes," the professor said. "I sat here alone in my office one night and brooded over it until I could stand it no longer. I was left with no choice. I had to dismiss Jeff."

She stared at him. "And you allowed my uncle to hire him?"

"I privately told your uncle about the incident," the professor said. "Benjamin preferred to believe that somehow one of the other assistants had gotten to the books. He refused to accept the fact that Jeff was guilty and hired him. And until you brought me this news of books being stolen from Benjamin's collection, I was beginning to think I'd been wrong about Jeff."

"You must surely still be," she protested.

"I find the evidence strongly against him," he said.

"I'm sure there must be some other explanation," Clare protested.

"For your sake, and for Jeff's, I hope there is," Professor Curtis said. "But because I feel I need to give you any protection I can, I had to tell you the truth."

"The truth as you see it."

He shrugged. "What I believe to be true, if you like."

She said, "I'm sure you meant well. But I prefer to forget I have heard anything you said."

He came to her and touched her arm gently. "Forgive me. I hope you won't hate me for this. I merely am concerned about you."

Clare gave him a challenging glance. "And you were also upset by the news that there had been thefts of volumes you expected to be given to the university?"

Professor Curtis looked embarrassed. "The information did bother me."

"You are as much obsessed with books as Uncle Benjamin or any of the others."

"I would imagine I am."

She sighed. "Thank you for trying to help. Now I think I must go."

"I fear I've offended you."

"Worried me," she said. "I'll have to admit that. But I know you said what you did in my best interests."

"Thank you," he said. "Please continue to believe that."

"I will," she said, anxious to get away from him and the room and all that was now linked in her mind with his indictment of Jeff. The visit to the university had been a mistake on her part.

Professor Curtis escorted her to the elevator and gave her instructions how to get the receptionist on the lower floor to secure a cab. He talked to her in a fatherly fashion, but she hardly heard what he said. His accusations against Jeff, on top of everything else, had hit her with shattering impact.

"I will come by as soon as I can to see your uncle," the professor promised as she stepped into the waiting elevator.

"Thank you," she said. Her last glimpse of him as the elevator door closed was of a man gravely upset. She knew that he felt he had spoken too frankly to her.

Downstairs, she spoke to the girl at the reception desk, and after a wait that seemed endless, the taxi came. She gave the driver the address on Mount Vernon Street and sank back, exhausted. She kept her eyes closed for most of the drive. All the time she was wondering if the professor could possibly be right and how she was going to face Jeff.

She was still in the same grim mood when she reached the house. She paid the cab and quickly ran up the stairs. When she entered the foyer, she was greeted by Winifred coming down the stairway.

Winifred asked her, "Where have you been?"

"At the university to see Professor Curtis," Clare said. "I left word where I was going."

"No one told me," Winifred said coldly, her hand on the railing of the stairway.

"I'm sorry," Clare apologized. Sensing something unusual in the older woman's manner, she asked, "Is anything wrong?"

"You uncle's condition has changed," Winifred said.

Clare took a step forward. "Is he worse?"

"No," Winifred said. "As a matter of fact, he is a little better. Dr. Greensmith is up there with him now. I sent for him."

"What happened?"

"Something very strange," the older woman said. "He managed to speak. He said just one word."

"That's wonderful news!" Clare exclaimed. "What was the single word he said?"

Winifred frowned. "It was a name."

"A name?"

"Yes. François."

"François? Do you recall his knowing anyone by that name?"

The dark-haired woman nodded solemnly. The eyes behind her glasses held a strange glint. She said, "François Duval. That was the name of the young man who was shot and killed while trying to prevent the Book of Gospels from being stolen."

"Oh!" Clare said, shocked.

"The killing has always weighed heavily on

Benjamin's mind," Winifred said. "I suppose he was thinking about it, and that is why he spoke that unfortunate young man's name."

"Possibly," she said. "But why should he remember now? It happened so long ago."

Winifred came down the remaining steps to stand with her in the foyer. She said, "Perhaps because his mind is in a muddled state as a result of the stroke. The subconscious is taking over and speaking for him."

"And that was all he was able to say?"

"Yes."

Clare asked, "Is Jeff back yet?"

"He's in the library," the older woman said.

Just then Dr. Greensmith came down the stairs. Seeing them, he nodded and came down to join them. He seemed in a baffled state of mind.

"A most unusual case," he told Winifred. "The nurse agrees with you that he did manage to utter that one word. Then he slipped back into his completely paralyzed state. Oh, there is a little movement in the eyes, but it is minimal. I would have expected the improvement to have continued."

Clare spoke up, "You would normally expect him to say a few words more and be able to continue speaking?"

"His speech should remain at that level," the bald doctor agreed. "Even though it might be incoherent, or come at long intervals, I'd think that once he had managed a word, he would manage others."

Winifred sighed. "It's a sad business!"

"A perplexing case," the doctor admitted. He turned to Clare. "Thank you for filling in so well last night. I have been able to get a nurse for tonight and from now on. So I may not have to impose on you again."

"I was glad to do it," she said.

Dr. Greensmith smiled at her. "That is the proper spirit." He turned to Winifred and added, "I want you to consider what I told you earlier about having your husband moved to a hospital. This business we've just been through seems to me to make it even more urgent he should have the group care only a hospital can offer."

Winifred's face clouded. "I'll think about it, Doctor. I make no promises."

"I want you to consider it carefully," the doctor said.

He and Winifred moved toward the door, still talking. Clare hurried up the stairs to the library on the second floor.

Jeff was up on a ladder, placing books back on an upper shelf, when she entered the sunlit library. Seeing her, he at once left the books in a stack on the top of the ladder and came down to her.

"I've been worried about you," he said.

"I just went to the university," she told him.

"So Mrs. Fox told me. But why?"

"Professor Curtis wanted to talk to me."

Jeff frowned. "He must have had something very important to say to drag you all the way out to the university."

"Not really," she said, defensive and watching him for any unusual signs of sullenness or guilt. "I felt I wanted to talk to him. I was glad to go."

He sighed and stood there studying her grimly. "I kept thinking of that old man with the dark glasses and feeling sure you'd stumbled into some sort of trap."

"I was never alone," she said. "I took a taxi both ways."

"At least that was smart."

"I did as you suggested."

Jeff asked her, "Have you heard about your uncle?"

"His managing to speak?"

"Yes."

"Yes. I think it may be very significant."

Jeff eyes widened. He said, "I doubt if you have any clue as to just how significant it is."

"Tell me," Clare said.

The young man looked excited. "You heard what he said? The one word? A name!"

"François."

"Right. And you know to whom he was referring?"

"François Duval, the young man who had your job and was shot and killed."

"That's correct," Jeff went on excitedly. "So don't you get the link?"

She stared at him in perplexity, "What link?"

"Between François Duval and the Nun of Valencia. Last night your uncle was terrified by the visitation of the ghost. It must have started a train of thought in his mind. He recalled the young man's murder being put down to the curse following the Book of Gospels. Then when the nun showed herself again last night, your uncle knew the curse was about to take its toll from you."

Clare was fascinated by this explanation. She said, "Uncle Benjamin was very frightened. You could see it in his eyes."

"And it was sheer terror that allowed him to gasp that name a little while ago," Jeff said confidently. "The doctor doesn't understand, but I do."

"You may be right," she said hesitantly.

"I know I am. Now Benjamin has lapsed back into a near-coma."

"Should you tell Winifred what you think?" she worried.

"No," he said. "What thanks would she give me?"

"I'm only thinking she might pass the information on to the doctor, and it would help him in treating my uncle."

Jeff gave her a cynical look. "Neither Winifred nor the doctor would believe me. It would be a waste of time."

"If your theory is correct," she said, "it means that I really did see a ghost last night."

"I doubted it," Jeff admitted. "Now I'm ready to change my opinion."

"You were very dubious last night," she said.

"So I made a mistake."

"It's all terribly confusing," she said, moving by him to stare out the window. "And we still don't know where that old man with the dark glasses fits in!"

Jeff came over by her. "Try and get him out of your mind. He's some kind of mental case. Be thankful if you never see him again."

She glanced at Jeff over her left shoulder. "I'm not to be used as a nurse again tonight."

His eyebrows raised. "They have someone else?"

"Yes. Dr. Greensmith has a regular nurse coming on duty."

"Aren't you glad?"

"Yes and no."

Jeff's smile was wryly amused. He said, "I'm finding it hard to get proper answers from you today."

"I didn't mean to seem evasive," she said, blushing.

"That's how it comes out," he warned her.

"I try to be subtle," she said. "And I don't do well at it."

"I'll accept that explanation," he said.

She turned and seated herself wearily in a plain chair by the window. Looking up at him, she said, "You worked with Professor Curtis once, didn't you?"

"Yes. Why?"

"He told me about it today."

"What did he tell you?" Jeff asked almost belligerently.

"Nothing much," she said. His sudden tenseness was frightening her. She realized that the professor might have been telling her the truth: that Jeff was a neurotic thief. He was surely behaving suspiciously now.

"I'd wager he told you a lot," Jeff insisted. "Let me have the gory details."

Clare eyed him solemnly. "He said that you were an excellent assistant. And I asked him why he let you go and take a private job with my uncle."

Jeff's eyes were hard. "Well?"

"He said you appeared tired of university work."

"Did he actually say that?"

"Yes."

The young man said thinly, "That isn't true."

"Isn't it?"

"No. I left the university because he no longer wanted me. He dismissed me, or at least asked me to offer my resignation. Your uncle was very annoyed by what the professor did. And as soon as I was free, he hired me."

"Why didn't Professor Curtis want you at the university?" she asked.

"I've never really been able to understand," he

said with a frown. "I did a thorough job, perhaps too thorough. In the end he may have become jealous of me."

"Is that possible?"

Jeff laughed bittterly. "You don't know academic politics, or you wouldn't ask that."

"Professor Curtis strikes me as being a mild, fair man," she protested.

"He is also very deep. There are protective coverings which he rarely lets down. Don't ever think you truly know him. You won't."

She stared at the young man she had come to love and said, "You sound so bitter. I took it for granted that you and the professor were friends."

"We are, I suppose."

"You don't sound it," she chided him.

He gave her a questioning look. "Did he sound to you as if he were my friend?"

She knew this brought crimson to her cheeks. It was impossible to hide this evidence of a guilty conscience. She faltered. "I can't say that he sounded as vindictive as you."

"But he did tell you that he'd dismissed me from the university."

"He hinted at it."

Jeff's expression was bitter. "I think that's why he had you up there: to try to turn you against me."

"Don't be ridiculous!" she protested. "I went up there to discuss last night and Uncle Benjamin."

"It seems you didn't have much time for those subjects, since you were so busy dissecting me," he told her.

"That's not fair!" she said.

"I'm sorry," Jeff apologized. "I happen to be more than a little touchy about the university. Having that job meant a lot to me."

"More than this one?"

"No," Jeff said, his manner changing as his tone became warmer. "I have great personal admiration for your uncle, and I've enjoyed working for him. And through being here, I came to meet you."

"So you did," she said with a wry smile.

"And that is the most important thing in my life so far," he assured her earnestly.

"Yet you find no difficulty in accusing me of talking about you behind your back with the professor," she reminded him.

He looked hurt. "I didn't mean that."

She was on her feet. "It sounded as if you did."

"I've told you I'm sorry," Jeff said contritely. "Leaving Bedford University under a cloud was bad for me and for my career. If it hadn't been for your uncle, I might be still looking for a job."

"I see," she said.

"I think Professor Curtis was jealous of me and unfair, but I'll say no more."

"Perhaps it would be just as well if you didn't," she agreed. "Uncle Benjamin has spoken once; perhaps it's only a beginning. He may soon regain complete power of speech, and then he'll be able to clear up some of the mystery."

"I certainly hope so," Jeff said.

She glanced at her wristwatch and saw it was nearly four. "It's getting late," she said. "You won't need me here for anything today, will you?"

"No, not today," he said.

"Then I'll go up to my room and rest for a while," she said.

She started out, then paused to turn and ask him, "By the way, about the missing books: have you found any others gone today?"

Jeff looked terribly guilty. "No," he said awkwardly. "I haven't. I really haven't taken any check today."

"I wondered," she said quietly.

Jeff followed her to the door. "I will look around later. I had some complicated banking to do that took the entire morning."

"I'll see you at dinner," she said.

CHAPTER ELEVEN

Clare was still in a confused state of mind as she entered her bedroom. Her talk with Jeff had been a good deal less than satisfactory, and the single word her uncle had said had added to the mystery of the ghostly attacker rather than solved it. She closed the door after her and started across the room to the closet to change into her dressing gown.

All at once she had a feeling there was another presence in the room. It came to her in a sudden flash, and she stood in the center of the bedroom, fear crossing her pretty face. Why did she have this strange sensation of evil, of the supernatural! She glanced about her nervously, and as she scanned the room her eyes touched the dresser, and what she saw there sent a cold chill down her spine.

In the middle of the dresser was an open book. It had not been there before, she was sure of that! And after the first moment of shock she went over to the book. It was ancient, with a leather binding. Her hands trembled slightly as she lifted it to see its title. It was "Murders Unsolved." She checked the pages at which it had been opened and saw that it was at the beginning of a chapter entitled, "Murder of a Beauty."

She snapped the book shut and stared at it in dismay. Was it there as a crude warning? Or had someone placed it on the dresser as a perverse joke? She couldn't decide which. She had no idea who could have been responsible. But one thing did seem obvious to her. Jeff ought to know something about the old book.

With the book in her hands, she made her way down the two flights of stairs to the library level. Jeff was still in the book-lined room. He was seated at his desk as she entered.

She went directly to him and showed him the book. "Do you recognize this?"

He at once got up and took it from her. He was clearly stunned. "Where did you get it?" he demanded. "It is one of the missing books."

"It was in my room," she said grimly, "and on my dresser, opened at the chapter called 'Murder of a Beauty.' Do you think it had some meaning for me?"

He was still holding the book and looking shocked. "I don't understand it," he said. "This was one of the first books I missed, and now it turns up in your room."

"Do you want to blame that on the ghost as well?" she asked with a hint of sarcasm.

"It must have been put there to frighten you," he said. "But by whom and to what purpose?"

"I can't supply you with any answers," she said.

"Whoever stole the books also wanted to be rid of you," Jeff said, giving her a troubled look. "I'd say it still adds up to Winifred or someone working with her."

Clare sighed. "It seems we discussed that before."

"It still may be true."

"I doubt if we'll ever prove it," she said.

"Whoever it was went to your room while you were out and did this," Jeff said. "And they had a definite purpose in doing it. I would say the suspects have to be narrowed down to those in the house. And that doesn't give us too many."

She said, "At least you've got one of your books back."

"Yes. I wonder where the others are," he mused, staring at the book again.

"Whoever put that in my room could undoubtedly tell you," she said.

"I'd imagine so," he said in a taut voice.

"I thought you should see it," she said as she turned to leave.

"Thanks," he said.

She left him still studying the book and started up the stairs to her room once again. As she reached the third landing, Winifred came from the direction of the sickroom. The dark-haired woman was showing the strain of the ordeal she was undergoing.

Pausing before Clare, she said, "I think I should get out of the house for my evening meal. Let us go to Pierre's."

"Only if we go and come back together," Clare told her. "I'm terrified of that old man with the dark glasses. And he nearly always seems to be there for dinner. He has rented the basement apartment from Pierre."

"I know," Winifred said. "I'll be ready to leave in a quarter-hour."

"That will give me time to change," Clare said. She liked the idea of having an early dinner, and it would be nice to have company. She hurried upstairs, washed and changed her clothes.

Winifred was waiting for her when she went back down. The dark-haired woman said, "The nurse who just came on duty thinks that Benjamin's color and general appearance is better. I hope she's right!"

"She'd probably notice it more quickly than we would, " she told the older woman.

"That's what I felt," Winifred agreed.

They left the old house and went next door to Pierre's. It was well-filled with early diners, and the proprietor greeted them with a smile and took them to their usual table.

"And how is the *monsieur?*" he wanted to know.

"We think he's better," Winifred told him.

"Ah, that is good," Pierre said agreeably. He then gave them menus and went on his way.

"How long has this restaurant been here?" Clare asked her uncle's wife.

"It opened not long after we established our regular residence on Mount Vernon Street," Winifred said. "It was a few months before we met Pierre and Madame Reaux. We used to dine at the Parker House before we began coming here. But that was some distance away, and the dining room has changed lately."

"So you became regular patrons here."

"Yes," Winifred said. "I must say we spent many happy hours in this restaurant. Pierre and his wife run it well."

"They seem to get good crowds."

"Madame Reaux spends most of her time in the kitchen," the older woman said. "But she is a charming person. You know; you've had brief conversations with her."

"Yes. She has a sad air."

The waiter came and they ordered, then talked some more as they awaited dinner.

Clare felt it might be a good opportunity to ask her uncle's wife a few questions about Jeff. She began by saying, "Whom did my uncle employ before he hired Jeff?"

Winifred grimaced. "He had several people. None of them were satisfactory. François Duval had been with us so long he was excellent. None of the others did as well. But then Jeff became available, and he turned out to be almost as competent as François."

"He was at the university before he came with Uncle Benjamin, wasn't he?"

"Yes. He was assistant to Professor Curtis."

"Strange that he would leave such an important post for work in a relatively modest private library," Clare said, hoping that Winifred would come forth with some revealing remark.

Winifred looked thoughtful. "I've wondered about that."

"Did my uncle ever comment on it?"

"No. He was strangely silent about hiring Jeff. I guess he felt it was none of my business. I was surprised when he got him from the university."

"I should think so," Clare said, leading her on.

"My private opinion," Winifred said, leaning across the table in a conspiratorial fashion, "is that the two didn't get along well. Professor Curtis saw that Jeff had great ability and at once became jealous of him."

"That's unfortunate."

"Yes. But I believe it to be true. I tried to sound Benjamin out on it, but he wouldn't commit himself. He is a great friend of Professor Curtis, and perhaps he didn't want to admit such a close friend had serious failings."

"Jeff seems an outstanding person," she said.

"I have some reservations about him," Winifred said with a return to her old arrogant manner. "But then there are few people who are perfect."

"That is true," Clare said.

Their food came, and for a while little else was said between them. They were having coffee and dessert when Clare looked up and saw the elderly gray-haired man with dark glasses coming down the aisle of the restaurant. He was wearing his usual shabby clothes and walking with a queer, shuffling gait. He passed by them and took a seat in a far corner.

Clare leaned over toward her uncle's wife and said, "That's him."

"Who?" Winifred asked blankly, seeming so naive Clare was convinced it was a deliberate pretense on the older woman's part.

"The man with the dark glasses. He's behind you and to the left. But don't look now."

"Is he the one you suspect might be a madman?" Winifred asked.

"Yes."

"Is he staring at us?" Winifred wanted to know.

Clare eyed him furtively. "I think so. It's hard to say with those dreadful glasses."

"I'm ready to leave," her uncle's wife said. "What about you?"

"I'd like to get out of here," Clare agreed.

As they left the restaurant, Winifred halted to ask Pierre, "What is the name of that man with the dark glasses?"

"*Monsieur* Morely," Pierre replied with a smile.

"You say he is a retired lawyer," she said.

"I believe so," Pierre said. "To be truthful, my wife looks after the renting of the apartments, and she knows much more about him than I do."

"I must speak with her about him when the

opportunity arrives," Winifred said sternly. "My niece finds him frightening."

Pierre looked worried. "But you shouldn't be afraid of him. *Monsieur* Morely is a very fine man, and a quiet one. Most nights find him at home reading."

"Thank you," Winifred said as they moved on.

In the house, Clare went directly up to the sick-room with Winifred. The nurse on duty stood back so they could stand by the bed and view the stricken Uncle Benjamin. His eyes were open again, and they found Clare and offered her a look of mute sorrow.

Winifred whispered, "He knows you. I'm sure of it."

"He seems to," Clare agreed. "I'd say he's much more himself than he was last night."

"I feel the same way," his wife replied.

Clare remained by the bedside of her Uncle Benjamin for longer than she had at any time except when she'd been acting as his nurse. And all the while she was there, those pleading eyes were fixed on her.

At last she felt she had to go. She said good night to the nurse and Winifred and went up to her room. She opened the door and went in. She was startled to find the lights on, and when she took a step inside she was further shocked by the spectacle of Jeff coming sheepishly out of her clothes closet.

"What are you doing in my room?" she demanded.

"I got back before you and thought I'd check around," the young man said.

Clare was indignant. "You hadn't my permission to come in here."

"I didn't think you'd mind, and your finding

that book in here got me interested," he apologized.

"Did you find anything more?"

"No," he said. "I'm sorry to say I didn't."

"You frightened me," she accused him.

"Evidently," Jeff said. He gave her a puzzled look. "You know, ever since you came back from the university today you've behaved oddly toward me."

"What made you think that?"

"Everything!"

"That's suitably vague!"

"You know what I mean," Jeff protested. "I don't like to come out with it frankly, but I'd say there was a general distrust in your manner."

"Indeed?" She pretended to be casual and amused by this.

"Yes. Come off it, Clare," he said. "What kind of poison did Curtis feed you about me?"

"You're imagining that."

"I don't think so," he said grimly. "I'd say he's filled you with malicious lies about me."

She met his troubled glance with a cool one of her own. "Do you have such a troubled conscience?"

He shook his head. "That question isn't like you."

"Sorry."

He gave a deep sigh and went over to the window to stare down at the lights of distant Charles Street moodily. "I don't know what it is about this house, but it destroys everything in the end; even the thing you and I found in each other."

In spite of her suspicions, she found herself touched by his genuine despair. She crossed over to him and placed a hand on his arm. "I'm sorry, Jeff," she said softly.

He turned to her. "Are you?"

She nodded. "Yes," she whispered.

Jeff put his arms around her and held her close. Then he touched his lips to hers.

When he released her, he said, "Let's get out of here, at least for an hour or so! There are a couple of coffee shops near here on Charles Street. We can walk to them and make the tour."

She smiled wanly. "If you think that would help."

"Anything to break the tension of this place," he said.

So she put on a topcoat, and they left the old house. It was cold outside, and she drew her coat tightly around her. Then she happened to look across to the opposite sidewalk and saw a familiar figure.

"Look!" She dragged at Jeff's arm.

"What?"

"Over there!"

Jeff glanced and in a wry voice said, "Your friend. Do you want me to challenge him?"

"No." She shuddered. "If he's crazy, there's no telling what he'll do. Let's hurry down to Charles Street."

Jeff nodded. "It will be interesting to see if he follows us."

They were filled with new tension as they made their way down the steep hill to the level of the Bohemian Charles Street. This was one of the main areas of hippie existence in Boston. Jeff knew all the various places, and they headed for the first of the coffee shops. It was a modest spot, located in an abandoned store, and it had a combined coffee shop and palmistry sign hanging out over it. In the window there was a huge outline of a hand divided in sections to indicate the regions of interest in palmistry. A curtain shielded the interior from the street.

As they hesitated at the entrance, she glanced down the street, and sure enough, the old man with the dark glasses was following them!

"He's back there," she whispered to Jeff. "He's pretending to be studying a store window, but he's been following us."

"So it seems," Jeff agreed with a drawn look on his handsome face.

They went into the coffee shop, which was dimly lighted and had shiny orange walls. The light fixtures were black, and so were the tables. The place was crowded with young people of both sexes with long hair. Smoke created a pattern of trailing blue in the air, and a sound system in the rear boomed out a rock beat.

Jeff gave her a pallid smile. "It's pretty grim, but at least it's a change."

"I used to love these places," she said. "I still think they're fun."

A glum young man in blue jeans found them a table, and they ordered cups of an exotic coffee. After that they amused themselves by studying the types around them and giving each other amused glances.

They stayed in the restaurant for almost an hour and a half. Then Clare decided it would be wise to move on. She gave Jeff a nod, and he paid the bill. In a moment they had left the loud noise, heat and smoke for the cold air of the street.

"Anyhow, it was a change," Jeff said.

"I know," she agreed. She was looking up and down the street anxiously. "I don't see any sign of him," she said.

"You sound disappointed," he joked with her.

"I can promise you I'm not!"

"I honestly think you've grown fond of your admirer in dark glasses," he went on to tease her.

"Don't believe it."

"Shall we go home?" he asked.

"Yes," she said. "I think so. It's not really late, but I'm tired."

"So am I," he said. "And you had that nursing ordeal all night."

"Uncle Benjamin should be in a hospital," she said, returning to a familiar theme. "I know it, but I can't persuade Winifred."

"She's a strange person," Jeff said.

They reached the house and went inside. No one seemed to be downstairs. The lights in the library had been turned out. She and Jeff went on up to the third floor and the sick room. They paused at the door and spoke briefly to the nurse in attendance on Benjamin Rand.

"He's sleeping," the nurse said. "And Mrs. Rand has gone to bed."

"I think we'll follow her example," Clare told the nurse.

Jeff accompanied her upstairs and kissed her good night at her door. "It wasn't a bad evening," he said.

"I enjoyed it," she told him.

Clare quickly prepared for bed. Tonight she was really exhausted from both an emotional and physical standpoint. She turned off the bedside lamp, pulled the clothes up over her and settled down to sleep with a sigh. It was not surprising that sleep came to her almost at once. But with the sleep came a series of weird dreams.

The gray Nun of Valencia was in her bedroom, crouching in the shadows, watching her from the protective folds of her hood. Then the phantom turned and left the room and went downstairs.

The scene quickly flashed to the library. Jeff was stretched out on the floor, just as she'd found her uncle. There was blood over his white shirt front, and he was unconscious. Bending over him with a knife in her hand, ready to strike him again, was the Nun!

Clare screamed out to stop the assault on the man she loved, and with the scream she woke up. At once her thoughts turned to the library and to Jeff. She was suddenly certain that something was wrong down there!

She switched on her bedside lamp and put on her robe and slippers. Then she made her way to the door and went out into the hall. The house was still deathly quiet as she started slowly down the stairs. She reached the third floor and saw the small glow of light from the sickroom door.

Then she went on down to the library level. As she reached the second landing, she hesitated in the shadows. The library was still in darkness. She crossed the landing to the library door and stood there.

As she did so, there was the beam of a flashlight suddenly focused on one of the shelves of books. She was able dimly to make out the hunched figure holding the light. She screamed, and the intruder wheeled around and turned the beam of the light full on her with a blinding effect—but not so quickly that she hadn't a glimpse of him and recognized the old man with the dark glasses!

CHAPTER TWELVE

Clare screamed, and as she did so the man with he dark glasses sprang at her and struck her with he flashlight. It was a stunning blow, and she lumped to the floor. As she lay there trying to lear her head, he struck her again. She managed . whimper of fear and tried to drag herself safely ff in the darkness.

Then suddenly the room was flooded with light, nd Jeff appeared in robe and pajamas. The young brarian quickly took in the situation and made or the elderly man in the dark glasses. The inruder shied away from him with surprising agilty and started out. He had almost reached the oor before Jeff caught him with a flying leap that ook them both to the hardwood floor of the brary.

Clare was recovering now and struggled to a tanding position, her eyes fixed on the fierce attle taking place between the two on the floor. he heard other voices, and a glance told her that Vinifred, Mrs. Fox and the nurse were all athered in the doorway, watching the melee with arious degrees of astonishment and apprehenon.

The man in the dark glasses was fighting back furiously, and it took all of Jeff's strength and ability with his fists to hold his own. Jeff finally got the man on the floor under him and, straddling him, delivered some punishing blows to his face which left his opponent unconscious.

Then Jeff ripped off the battered hat from the motionless man's head, and with it came the gray wig. He next stripped him of the glasses, and an incredulous Clare found herself staring at the round face of Professor Alan Curtis! The placid face was puffy and swollen, but there was no question as to who it was.

Jeff got up from his knees, his own face bloody and battered, and gave her a grim look. "See what's turned up!" he said.

After that everything fused into a blur of confusion in Clare's mind. There was Winifred angrily accusing the professor and blaming him for attacking her husband. It was a loud, shocking scene.

She was aware of Jeff urging the distraught woman to return to her room. And then he helped a beaten Professor Curtis to an easy chair to await the arrival of the police. The professor carefully avoided their eyes and sat sullenly in the chair, his head bent.

Plain-clothes men from the nearby Boston Police station arrived, and Jeff made the initial charges against his former employer. Then Professor Alan Curtis made an exit in a dejected silence between two stern plain-clothes men.

Mrs. Fox brought them coffee, and Clare felt somewhat better. The word was that her Uncle Benjamin had slept through the entire fracas, unaware of what had taken place in the library. Jeff went and fixed up his face and returned, cleaned but with band-aids affixed at strategic spots to cover the cuts and bruises inflicted on him by the professor.

Clare was sitting slumped in an easy chair in the drawing room with a half-empty cup of coffee in her hands when he came in to join her. He was still in his robe and pajamas and showed the ordeal he'd been through.

He sank down in a divan beside her and said, "Well?"

She shook her head in a puzzled fashion. "I just don't know."

"I'm pretty confused myself."

She gave him a troubled look. "What does it mean?"

"In the simplest terms, Professor Curtis is a book thief. His love of books has twisted his character."

"It's frightening." she said. "I never thought of him as our enemy. And I never guessed that he was the old man with the dark glasses. I spent a half-hour at the university telling him about the madman who'd been following me. He must have been secretly laughing all the while."

Jeff frowned. "It's not as simple as that. He was too deeply involved in criminal activities to have found it funny."

"Why?"

He said, "This has been going on for a long while. He's been stealing books and either hoarding them or selling them on the black market to collectors as avaricious as himself; men who will pay tremendous sums just to possess book treasures and hide them away."

"He was infected with the same madness."

"Without a question," Jeff said. "And it didn't start here. It began at the university. I didn't want to tell you before. But at the time I was there, a number of books vanished. I think he dismissed me deliberately to give the impression I had been to blame."

"Of course he did," Clare said. And then, her cheeks crimsoning, she confessed, "He even told me about the missing books and hinted that you were responsible and that you probably were to blame for the books that were vanishing here."

Jeff eyed her grimly. "That sounds like him. Clever as a fox! Or perhaps cunning is the more proper term. He was using his first offense against me to protect himself in this new series of thefts and proposed ultimately to blame me."

"I'm sure of it, she said.

"To be able to get into the house, he rented the basement apartment next door and assumed a disguise. It was another red herring. He was diverting our attention from himself and having us watch an entirely fictitious character whom he could dispose of at any time. If he didn't succeed in placing the blame for the book thefts on me, he could make sure we blamed this fictitious Mr Morely, the ex-lawyer."

"The Reauxs could never have guessed what he was up to," she said.

"No. He made them his innocent accomplices. Once he got that basement apartment, he was in business. I suspect there is a secret passage between the other house and this, and he probably used it. That eliminated any problems about getting in here."

Clare was stunned by it all. "And so he went about his thefts, while trying to build up the fictitious character by behaving suspiciously and following me around."

"He succeeded," Jeff said. "It's the old ma

gician's trick of misdirection. We weren't even thinking about the professor; we were much too interested in the man with dark glasses."

Clare sighed. "And he invited me to the university to talk to sound me out; to find if his scheme was going over and also to plant suspicions in my mind about you being the thief."

"Don't forget that," Jeff warned her. "It's an example of how wily he was."

"What about the ghost?"

"It wouldn't surprise me if somewhere in his apartment we found the gray habit of the Nun of Valencia. Once he'd donned it, who could tell whether the phantom was a man or woman? And he always encouraged the theory of the ghost."

"True," she said.

"If you hadn't come down here tonight and caught him red-handed, he might well have gotten away with it."

"That's true," she said.

Jeff stared at her. "What made you come down?"

Embarrassed, she said, "A dream, believe it or not! I had a dream that you were down here, being threatened by the phantom. I saw blood on your shirt as you lay on the floor, and the Nun of Valencia was bending over you with a knife poised to strike you mortally."

Jeff smiled bleakly. "Well, before it was over you did see blood on my face and shirt."

"It was awful!"

"I know," he said.

Another phase of the problem came to mind, and she asked him, "Do you think that Winifred was right: that the night my uncle had his stroke, it was brought about by finding the professor in the library stealing from him?"

"It could well be," Jeff said. "It's only speculation, of course. Unless and until your uncle is able to talk we won't really know what happened."

"Still, I think it is likely," she said with a frown. "You can imagine what a shock it must have been for him to find his trusted friend in the process of robbing him."

"It seems logical," Jeff said.

"What now?"

"I don't know," he admitted. "The professor will be charged with theft, breaking into a private home and assault. That ought to take care of him. He'll surely lose his position at the university, and it is extremely unlikely he'll be able to get another."

She gave a tiny shudder. "Just that single flaw has ruined his life."

"It happens all too often," Jeff said wearily. "In many ways I have the utmost respect and admiration for him. But he has become a man obsessed. And when our passions rule us, we become a danger to society. And society is never slow to protect itself."

"At least not in cases like his," she said somewhat bitterly. "The larger threats are beyond dealing with, it seems."

"Which makes retaliation all the more vicious for an offender like Alan Curtis," Jeff said. "He'll get a short prison term and then, unless he has enough private funds, he'll wind up a faceless clerk in a rare book store in some large city of the world. At least he'll be close to his one passion."

"He had so much, it seems a pity," she said.

"The greed became too great for him to handle," Jeff told her. "And I can't offer him that much pity. He was ready to destroy me for his own purposes. And in a way, that also meant ruining your chances of happiness."

She reached out and touched his hand with hers. "I don't think I ever reached the point where I was ready to turn away from you."

"That was not his fault," Jeff said.

"Do you think we'll ever find the missing books?"

"I don't know. He wouldn't talk to me before he left. He wouldn't say anything."

"So unless the police locate them in his apartment or learn where he sold them, the volumes are hopelessly lost."

"I'm afraid so," Jeff said.

"Perhaps they are in the apartment he rented next door," she suggested.

"The police have already been in there. But tomorrow I'll ask Madame Reaux's permission to visit the apartment and search it on my own."

"That might turn up some of the books," she agreed. "The police wouldn't really be looking for them at this point."

So it came about that the next afternoon they called on Madame Reaux. The melancholy Frenchwoman and her husband looked shocked and worried about all that had happened. Pierre Reaux was extravagantly apologetic, and his wife seemed lost in a grim silence.

Jeff told them, "We would appreciate going through the apartment for two reasons. One, we think there may be some valuable books which the professor hid there. And also, we have an idea there may be a secret passage between the basement apartment and Benjamin Rand's house."

Madame Reaux shook her head. The dark circles under her sad eyes were more noticeable than ever. She said, "There is no secret passage. I papered the walls and closets of all the basement rooms. I would know if such were the case."

"Perhaps," Jeff said. "But it is possible ther may be books hidden down there."

"Books, yes," the woman agreed. "Pierre wil give you the key."

"The man was a rogue," Pierre lamented "Never have we been so utterly deceived."

The entrance to the basement apartment wa from a separate door below the street level whic had once been the service entrance. Pierre led th way down the several stone steps and laboriousl inserted the key in the lock. He opened the doo and beckoned them to follow him into the apart ment. It was of good size, although the ceiling were low and Madame Reaux had done an exce lent job of painting and papering it.

Pierre bowed respectfully. "I shall leave you tw here. My wife and I have to provide for the eve ning trade."

"Thank you," Jeff said. Then he turned to Clare "Let's go through everything."

The task did not prove as formidable as the might have expected. The apartment was clea and there wasn't too much furniture in it. It soo became obvious that Professor Alan Curtis ha only spent short periods in the place in his fals identity. Consistent with Madame Reaux's stat ment they found no secret passage. But in a smal dark storageroom, they did come upon seven o the missing books.

It seemed enough to justify the time and effor spent on the search. Jeff was so delighted at loca ing the missing volumes that Clare began to worr a little that he might be more infected with th hunger of collecting than he guessed. They gav the keys back to the Reauxs and took the book home.

Winifred came to the library to view the r

covered volumes with an air of impatience. "I can't feel excited over getting them back," she said. "Not when I know that they were the cause of my husband's present condition."

"You're only assuming that," Jeff protested.

"I'm positive of it," the dark woman said, her eyes flashing angrily behind her glasses. "Benjamin came into the library and found that awful Curtis man in the act of robbing him. They had an argument. Curtis struck him down, and poor Benjamin suffered his stroke."

Clare pointed out, "You're making a very simple case of it. Can you really be that sure?"

"I am," Winifred declared sternly.

Clare knew there would be no point in carrying on the debate with the woman. Once she made up her mind, it was hard to change it. So she said nothing more.

Jeff said, "At least you have recovered material worth many thousands of dollars." He knew Winifred valued books mostly for their monetary worth.

Winifred said reluctantly, "At least that is something. And if I have my way, Bedford University will never see one of Benjamin's books." And she went out.

When she was safely out of hearing, Jeff grimaced and told Clare, "That's another battle you may find yourself involved in. Your uncle's will is already made, giving the books to the university. There could be a horrendous court battle."

Clare sighed. "Let's hope it doesn't come to that."

She went up to her room in the late afternoon for a nap. She'd been up most of the night and was very weary. She also wanted to try to sort out her thoughts. In the excitement of capturing Professor

Curtis, almost all attention had been turned from the phantom who had stalked her several times in the old mansion.

It was Jeff's opinion that Professor Curtis might also have played the role of the Nun of Valencia. Surely he had done all he could to perpetuate the legend. He'd used it neatly to cover his own misdeeds. She fell asleep thinking about this, and so her dreams were filled with grim visions of the menacing figure in the gray habit.

She awoke to a knocking on her door. When she got up and opened the door, she discovered Winifred standing there. "I'm sorry to wake you," the older woman said. "But Dr. Greensmith has just phoned in and said the night nurse is ill. He wants to know if you'll take over as you did before."

"I suppose so," Clare said, though she really wasn't anxious to take on the task. Still, she couldn't see her uncle neglected. Again, she thought how senseless it was to keep him in the house rather than have him in a good hospital.

Winifred said, "Then I'll phone him back and tell him you'll take over the night shift."

"Yes," Clare said. "You can."

The dark woman hesitated, then said quickly, "I want you to know I'm grateful for what you've done. There are times when I'm less gracious than I should be. I can't help it. I'm a very nervous person. I hope you understand."

Clare was surprised at this sudden avalanche of gratitude on the part of her uncle's wife. She said quietly, "It's all right. Uncle Benjamin is very close to me. I want to do all I can to bring him back to health."

It was in this spirit that she went to the sickroom that night at eleven. She and Jeff had sat for a while in the drawing room discussing their plans for the future. Neither of them had felt like leaving the house. Now Jeff had gone up to his bedroom, and she was taking over the eight-hour vigil with her Uncle Benjamin until the morning nurse arrived.

Before leaving, the nurse told her, "He's been just a little restless, but I'm sure it's nothing to worry about."

Clare took her place by the bedside. Her uncle's skin seemed to have taken on the waxen tone of a permanent invalid's in the past week. He lay there with his eyes open, staring up into the shadows of the room. He seemed almost unaware of her presence.

Tho hum of the electric clock on the dresser was the loudest sound within her hearing. She felt she could almost hear its bearings turning. She'd not fortified herself with anything to read and decided she should get herself something. But she didn't want to leave the stricken man so soon after the change of nurses. She was positive he was aware of much more that went on around him than they guessed.

An hour passed. Her uncle's eyes had closed. Perhaps he was asleep. At least he was resting. The clock showed ten minutes after twelve. She decided the time had come for her to get a book or magazine. So she rose quietly from her chair and tiptoed out of the room. She hurriedly made her way down to the library on the floor below and secured several copies of magazines from the table on which incoming copies were kept.

Then she started up the dark stairway again. It amazed her that the old mansion still frightened her. There was an air of menace about it which remained. She could only wonder if they might have been mistaken after all, and if the Nun of

Valencia didn't exist as a phantom figure. It was too easy to say that Professor Alan Curtis had played this role as well as the one of the man with dark glasses.

As she reached the landing on which the sick-room was located, her fears increased. And she began to regret that she had left her uncle alone even for a few minutes. Helpless in his bed, he was a target for who knew what dark phantom? She hurried along the shadowy corridor and into the room, and then she halted and let out a shriek of fear!

For standing over her uncle with a knife poised to plunge into him was the familiar gray figure of the Nun of Valencia. For once Clare didn't allow her fears to immobilize her. She sprang at the ghost and dragged her back before the knife could find its mark in her uncle's chest.

And then, as she struggled with the phantom, a strange thing happened. Her Uncle Benjamin actually lifted himself up in his bed and called out hoarsely, "Clare! Save yourself!"

She heard no more. For at that instant the phantom plunged the knife in close to her shoulder blade. She felt a sharp pain, and then she blacked out. When she opened her eyes, she was on a bed in another room, and Jeff was sitting on the side of the bed watching her with troubled eyes.

"It's only a flesh wound," he told her. "Dr. Greensmith is on his way here."

She was still only vaguely aware of what was going on. She asked, "The phantom?"

"I came in time to take care of her," Jeff said grimly. "Another customer for the police."

Her eyes widened at this. "Who?"

"Madame Reaux."

"Madame Reaux!"

"Yes."

"Why?"

"Madame Reaux had an old score to settle. Her real name is Madame Duval. She's the mother of the young man who was employed in France by your uncle and who was killed defending his library."

Clare was shocked at this. She sat up in bed and winced from the pain of her stabbed shoulder. "She was the mother of François?"

Jeff nodded. "And since his murder, she has dedicated her whole life to revenging his death. She married again, and she and her husband came to Boston and bought the house next to your uncle. She set up the restaurant as a means of support, but her true ambition was to murder your uncle and others of his family. There was a secret passage from her basement apartment to this house, and she used it frequently."

"Where does Professor Curtis fit in?" she asked.

"He found out who she was and blackmailed her into allowing him to have the basement apartment and access to your uncle's library. It was an evil arrangement. She would allow him to steal from this house if he let her commit murder in it."

She gave Jeff a frightened look. "Then it was she whom my uncle discovered in the library and not Professor Curtis."

"Yes," Jeff said. "He found her lurking there in the guise of the Nun of Valencia. She revealed who she was and accused him of sacrificing her son for his books. Then she attacked him, and your uncle collapsed from a stroke."

"And he recognized her again the night she tried to stab me," Clare said. "That is why he finally managed the single word François. He was trying to tell us François' mother was in the house and playing the role of the vengeful nun."

"That's it," Jeff said grimly.

She lay back on the pillow weakly, then rose again almost at once. "Uncle Benjamin! When I was struggling with Madame Reaux, I was almost certain I heard him cry out a warning to me."

"You did," Jeff said. "Winifred is with him now, waiting for the doctor to come to attend to both you and him. He can move and say a few words."

"Then I didn't imagine it," she said.

"No. It looks as if the stress of that moment helped bring him out of the stroke. Let's pray the improvement lasts."

As it turned out, it did. Within a few months Benjamin Rand was back on his feet and able to look after his valuable collection of books. He was even able to give Clare away at her wedding in Trinity Church to Jeff. And Winifred played the surrogate role of mother of the bride so beautifully that Clare felt she must forever feel guilty for so misjudging the stern but basically good woman.

Then the big test came when Jeff was offered the post left vacant at Bedford University by the dismissal of Professor Alan Curtis. Jeff took his young bride up to the spacious office of the rare books division of the university where she'd been interviewed by the professor that afternoon.

Jeff gave her a questioning look. "Well, will I take it?"

"I don't know," she replied. She turned and stared at the portrait of the screen star glaring at them from the distant wall of the room. "I'd have to share you with so many people, including her. And then there are the books; your love will grow stronger for them as the years pass."

"I must plead guilty to that," he said; "it's a hazard of my profession. But if you love me and are a good wife, won't you allow me some human weaknesses?"

She smiled up at him. "So many times it is our weaknesses that make us different and interesting," she admitted. "Take the job! Just don't be another Professor Alan Curtis! Don't be unfaithful to me for a first edition." And she went into his arms.

Jeff smiled at her tenderly. "Never fear!" And he kissed her.

As he let her go, her eyes fell on an exquisite hand-wrought book of rare beauty on the desk beside them. She reached out and opened its cover. "Kleine Passion!" she exclaimed. "That's Nuremburg 1512 and illustrated with woodcuts by Albert Durer! It's priceless! How dare we stand here mooning over each other with all that beauty beside us neglected!"

Jeff gave a humorous groan. "I knew it! It's in your blood! You're bitten by the bug, too!"